THE LAST DAYS OF WOLF GARNETT

Clifton Adams

GUNSMOKE

First published in the UK by Hale

This hardback edition 2009
by BBC Audiobooks Ltd
by arrangement with
Golden West Literary Agency

ISBN 978 1 405 68255 8

British Library Cataloguing in Publication Data available.

Printed and bound in Great Britain by
CPI Antony Rowe, Chippenham and Eastbourne

THE LAST DAYS
OF
WOLF GARNETT

CHAPTER ONE

The stranger arrived in New Boston on the Tuesday stage from Gainsville. The driver handed down his warbag and saddle. "Big day for New Boston," the driver said, eying the crowd that milled on the plank sidewalks in front of the false-fronted stores.

The stranger mutely shouldered his saddle and bulled his way through the crowd of curious onlookers. A late-model Winchester under one arm, he went through the massed loafers with the unmindful arrogance of a war chariot going through light infantry. He had taken perhaps a dozen steps when he suddenly reached out and stopped a passing cowhand. "Which way to the sheriff's office?"

"Across the street." The cowhand pointed. "Over Rucker's feed store."

With not so much as a nod of thanks, the newcomer plowed across the deep-rutted street. He took the outside stairway to the second-floor gallery that overlooked the street. Two business offices had been built on top of the feed store, small boxlike affairs with single sash windows looking down on the colorless prairie town. There was a scaling sign beside the first door bearing the legend: *MARVIN DOOLIE, M.D.* In smaller letters, was the message:

TREATMENT AND CONSULTATIONS ON A CASH BASIS ONLY.
POSITIVELY NO CREDIT.

The stranger studied the sign for a moment and moved
onto the next door. *GRADY OLSEN*, announced the faded
lettering on the door. *SHERIFF, STANDARD COUNTY*.
The sign looked as if it had been there, unchanged, for a
long time. The stranger went in.

A large, slope-shouldered, balding man sat at an oilcloth-
covered table, laboriously writing in a tablet of ruled paper.
"Set down," he said without looking up. "I'll talk to you in a
minute."

The stranger eased his saddle and warbag to the floor
but held onto his rifle. "The name," he said flatly, "is
Frank Gault."

"Set down, Gault." The sheriff waved absently at a cane-
bottom chair and went on writing.

"I came about Wolf Garnett."

"Lots of folks did." There was a note of irritation in the
sheriff's voice. For the best part of an hour he had been
trying to compose a bounty claim for the express company.
It was the first bounty he had ever put in for, and it did
not come easy.

"Where is he?" the stranger asked in the same flat tone.

"Where's who?"

"Sheriff," Frank Gault said with a cold snarl, "if you're
deaf, just nod your head and I'll try to talk louder. If
you're simple-minded I'll look for your deputy and talk to
him."

The big lawman straightened up at the table and looked
at the stranger for the first time. He looked at him steadily,
unblinkingly, his gray plainsman's eyes as hard as bullets.
Sheriff Grady Olsen had been the chief lawman of Standard
County for as long as most of its citizens could remember.
He was not accustomed to strangers—or anybody at all, for
that matter—tramping uninvited into his office and telling

him to his face that he was deaf or simple-minded, or possibly both.

The small room, which served as the sheriff's office and living quarters, rang with hostility. Olsen quietly studied every detail of Gault's big-boned frame, his sun-cured face and hawkish features. He did not speak until he was sure that he could do it calmly. "What," he asked at last, "is this about Wolf Garnett?"

"I want to see him."

"That ain't likely. We buried him this mornin'."

"Dig him up."

The sheriff blinked once, slowly, like a faintly curious owl. "Why," he asked ponderously, "would I want to do a thing like that?"

"I don't think the man you buried was Wolf Garnett."

". . . I see." Sheriff Olsen crossed his arms across his vast chest and asked coldly, "If we didn't bury Garnett, who did we bury?"

"I don't know." Gault gestured impatiently. "Some drifter, maybe."

Olsen assumed an air of limitless patience. "Fine," he droned. "Well and good. We buried the wrong man. His sister identified him as Wolf Garnett. He was wearin' Wolf Garnett's clothes. His black butterfly boots and the Montana Stetson. He had Garnett's bone-handled .45 in his holster when he was found. Two first-class lawmen recognized the Colt and identified it as the one that Garnett always carried. By the way," he added softly, gazing at Gault's own .45 which he wore high up, pilgrimlike, on his right hip, "there's an ordinance in New Boston that disallows the wearin' of firearms—except maybe if you're a traveler just passin' through." He smiled what was probably the smallest smile that Gault had ever seen. "Gettin' back to the point here. Like I said, we got plenty reason to believe that we buried Wolf Garnett and nobody but Wolf Garnett. You say we didn't. Why?"

"I saw Garnett four days ago in the Creek Nation, in one of those honky-tonks just across the line from the Unassigned Lands."

The sheriff seemed to fall asleep with his eyes open. After several seconds of silence he sat a little straighter and asked, "You know Garnett? You'd seen him, before that time four days ago?"

". . . Yes."

There was something in the way he said it that caused the big lawman to squint. "When was that?"

"About a year ago." Gault's eyes lost their sharp focus. He seemed to be gazing at some invisible spot several inches above Olsen's head. "I was in the coach that Garnett and his bunch held up and robbed, over on the Trinity."

It had not happened in Standard County, but Olsen nodded, remembering the incident. Almost a thousand dollars in grass money—rent money that cowmen paid the Indians for the use of their pastureland—had been taken from the strongbox. And there had been something else. After the robbery the highwaymen had run off the team. The coach had overturned and one of the passengers had been killed.

"My wife," Gault said harshly, as if he had been reading the sheriff's mind. "Killed. For no reason at all. They already had the money." He continued to gaze at that invisible spot above Olsen's head.

The sheriff sat for what seemed a long while, saying nothing. Then he sighed to himself. The sound whistled through his teeth. "You better set down, Gault. Go back to the startin' mark and tell me about Wolf Garnett."

Gault ignored the chair. "I've already said everything there is to say. I saw him. He's alive."

"Tell me again just where it was you saw him."

"An illegal whiskey place on Little River. Just across the line from the Unassigned Lands."

"Did the place have a name?"

Gault gritted his teeth and made an obvious effort to hold his temper. "Places like that don't have names. The sharpshooter that ran it was called Marcus. He might of been part Indian."

"This man you saw that you thought was Garnett, how close was you to him at the time?"

"Close enough to know it was Garnett." Gault's eyes glittered.

"How close?" Olsen persisted.

Gault hesitated. "Maybe . . . maybe a quarter of a mile."

The sheriff sat up and grunted. "Quarter of a mile. Must of been a right good-sized honky-tonk."

"He wasn't *in* the honky-tonk," Gault said, his anger rising. "He was just leavin', on horseback. Goin' into a stand of timber." Until this moment he had been absolutely sure that the man he had seen had been Wolf Garnett. But now, facing the sheriff's bland smugness, he wasn't sure any more.

Olsen looked at him for several seconds. At last he said, "I'll let you talk to Doc Doolie. He's the one that laid Garnett out and got him ready for buryin'."

"I didn't come here to talk, I came to see the body."

"Mister," the sheriff said wearily, "the thing's done. He's buried, fair and legal. The coroner attended to him and made his report. The sister of the dead man identified him. A hundred folks from hereabouts, and newspapermen from as far away as the Nations, was here to see the plantin'. I can't go diggin' him up again just because you was late."

"My horse went lame up north of the Red, that's the only reason I'm late. I headed south the minute I heard that you'd found somebody you thought was Wolf Garnett."

"South from where?" Olsen asked sleepily.

Frank Gault forced himself to answer without shouting. "South from the Big Pasture where I lease some grass from the Comanches—or used to."

"Used to?"

"I sold my stock after . . ." His eyes became remote and cold. "I sold out about a year ago and went lookin' for Garnett."

The sheriff sighed, pushed his chair back from the table and got up. He lumbered over to the wall and pounded on it with a hairy fist. "Doc, get yourself in here a minute!" He returned to the table and sat down again.

"I told you," Gault said angrily, "I didn't come here to talk, I came to see."

"There ain't nothin' to see," the sheriff told him placidly. "Nothin' that wouldn't wrench your guts, anyhow. When we found the body it was lodged in some roots of a salt cedar, over on the Little Wichita. It had been in warm water maybe two weeks, Doc says, when we found it. Like I say, it wasn't nothin' pretty to look at by that time."

"Who found it?"

"I did."

"How'd *you* come to find the body?"

"Lookin' for horse thieves. Comanches, most likely. They like to raid across the Red every chance they get. That's what comes of havin' Quakers as Indian agents." He smiled lazily. "Poor Lo ain't as dumb as some might figger. He knows them Quakers ain't goin' to do anything to him just for stealin' a few white men's horses. But I guess you know about that, runnin' cattle in the Big Pasture."

A figure appeared in the sheriff's open doorway, and Olsen said, "Doc, this here's Frank Gault. Mr. Gault runs cattle on Comanche grass. Or used to. He claims he seen Wolf Garnett up in the Choctaw Nation about a week ago, alive and kickin', fit as you please."

"Creek Nation," Gault said. "Four days ago."

Doc Doolie was a wizened little brown nut of a man. He came into the room, peering up into Gault's face. "Seen Garnett's ghost, maybe. But not Garnett. Not four days ago. He's buried. I seen to it myself."

"How can you be so sure it was Garnett?"

The little doc glanced at Olsen and shrugged. "I admit he wasn't much to look at by the time I got him. But his sister identified him."

"How?"

"By his clothes. By his size and general appearance. The sheriff must of told you that. Besides all that, there was a scar on the back of his neck in the shape of a cross. Wolf's sister said her brother had a scar just like that."

"Lanced boil," Gault said, unimpressed. "Half the men in Texas carry cross-shape scars caused from lanced boils."

Doolie looked at him and said dryly, "So you're a doc as well as a lease cowman."

"I know what a lance scar looks like."

Sheriff Olsen held up a hand and said patiently, "All right, it's not much. But a lot of little things, and they all add up to Wolf Garnett." He spread his big hands on the oilcloth. "Sorry, Gault. I know how you feel—guess I'd feel the same way, in your place. But it's a fact you'll just have to get used to. Garnett's dead. There's nothin' you or anybody else can do about it now."

Gault made no effort to hide his anger and disgust. "Where is this sister of Garnett's that was so handy when it came to identifying the body?"

"She's back at the family place on the Little Wichita." Olsen's eyes narrowed and his voice became cooler. "And don't you go botherin' her, Gault. She's had a hard time these last few days. I don't want her bothered any more."

"Then let me look at the body."

The big lawman shook his head. "I can't do it. We got decent folks here in New Boston. We don't go diggin' up the dead."

Frank Gault's angular jaw set like concrete. "Then you won't help me?"

"I'll do better'n that, I'll give you some good advice. Let

it alone. What's done's done, and there's no way you can change it."

"I see." Slowly and deliberately, Gault slipped his Winchester under his arm and picked up his saddle and warbag. He got as far as the door when he turned and glanced back at the sheriff. "I wonder," he said, "if there happened to be a price on Wolf's head?"

Something happened behind those pale eyes, but Gault couldn't be sure just what it was. "Yes," the sheriff admitted, with no change in tone, "there was a reward. The express company that Wolf had robbed put up a five-hundred-dollar bounty. And there was a cattlemen's association up in Kansas that claimed Wolf had killed one of their detectives—they put up another five hundred."

One thousand dollars. Gault had known men who would do anything, including murder, for much less. "Who's doing the collecting?" he asked.

Sheriff Grady Olsen managed a small smile. "I am. Now, if you don't mind, Gault, I've got a letter to write."

Gault answered him with a smile of his own, as taut as a fiddle string and etched with acid. "Two five hundred dollar 'dead or alive' bounties, and you collect them. Now it's not hard to understand why you're not in too big a hurry to open up that grave."

•

Gault was not surprised to find there were no vacancies in New Boston's only hotel, due to the holiday atmosphere brought on by the funeral and burying of a famous outlaw. "Mister," the desk clerk beamed at Gault, "we ain't had a room for rent since before suppertime yesterday. Seems like the whole county's gathered here. Just to be able to say they was on hand when the famous Wolf Garnett was planted, I guess. You might try the wagon yard at the end of the street. If they ain't got a camp shack for rent, they might allow you to sleep in the loft."

As Gault was turning to leave, the clerk said, "Mister, maybe I ought to tell you somethin', for your own good. About that .45." He looked at Gault's wood-handled weapon. "We got an ordinance in New Boston against carryin' firearms. The sheriff don't like it."

Gault smiled his heatless smile. "What does the town marshal say about it?"

"Ain't got a town marshal, just the sheriff. And Dub Finley, that's Olsen's deputy."

Handy, Gault thought silently. A million-acre county, with only two lawmen to look over it. That kind of job called for strong men.

There was no problem finding the wagon yard. A group of men were gathered by the livery corral beside the barn. Town loafers, and a few visiting cowhands and farmers. Gault lowered his saddle to his hip as he moved in to see what it was that interested them. "What's the excitement about?" Gault asked a cowhand who was just leaving.

"Wolf Garnett's outfit," the cowhand told him. "His gun and the rig he was wearin' when the sheriff found him." He grinned and strolled away toward the nearest saloon.

Gault stood like stone for several moments. Then, without a word, he bulled his way through the crowd, oblivious of the hostile looks and the grumbling. He stood gazing down at the items of curiosity that so fascinated the citizens of Standard County.

"Them boots," someone was saying. "Only pair like those anywheres in the country. Hand-made by a saddler over at Fort Worth. Best money could buy—that was Wolf Garnett."

Gault lowered his saddle to the ground, knelt in front of the boots and inspected them minutely. They were white rimmed now and stained by their long soaking in gyp water, but Gault would have recognized them anywhere. Once they had been richly black, with fanciful butterflies stitched above the vamps. They had been soft and smooth and expensive, and they had somehow smacked of the arrogance that had possessed the man who had worn them. And there was the cartridge belt, also black and probably bench made to order, for Wolf Garnett had not been one to stint on the necessities of his calling. The bone-handled .45, cast in the same mold of a thousand other Colts, was somehow distinctive because it had belonged to Wolf Garnett. And the foreign-looking Montana Stetson with its narrow brim and four-sided crease.

Gaunt studied the items one by one with great care. There was no doubt that they were real and that they had belonged to Wolf Garnett. The outlaw had worn these very items on the day, not quite a year ago, when he had so casually and offhandedly murdered Martha Gault.

In the back of Gault's mind he heard someone saying, "Mister, is somethin' the matter with you?" There was just the beginning of uneasiness in the voice. "You ain't about to have a fit, are you?"

Gault did not know what kind of expression had been on his face, but it was clear that this group of idlers had found it disturbing, if not outright alarming. They had quietly and without a word, started backing away from him, as they might have backed away from a dog that had suddenly started foaming at the mouth. Gault looked at them without actually seeing them. Then he got slowly to his feet and picked up his saddle.

He found the hostler filling feed troughs in the rear of the barn. "Have you got anything in the way of a camp shack for rent?" Gault asked him.

The hostler, a gimpy, buckshot-eyed little man of undeterminable age, was instantly alert and oozing greed. "Might be," he said cautiously. "How many of you?"

"Just myself. Tonight, and maybe tomorrow. I don't know how much longer."

"Won't come cheap," the little man warned him.

Gault made an inaudible sound in his throat and then gestured to indicate that the expense was of no importance. He owned no cattle now, no home, no land, no roots. But he did have money enough to see him through the next few months. After that it didn't matter.

Gault's shack was one of several green lumber boxes that had been built against the side of the barn to catch the overflow from the hotel on Saturdays and holidays. And days like today. Gault washed up at the livery pump. His face felt numb as he sloshed it with cold water. His insides felt numb too. And had for a long time.

He went to his shack, which was just big enough to hold the pole-and-rope bunk, and a few clothing pegs on the wall. There was no stove and no provision for one. Well, it was April, and the weather was mild in Texas. And there was an open fireplace next to the pump for guests who wanted to do their own cooking.

Gault sat on the bunk and began emptying the cartridges from the magazine of his Winchester. When the magazine was empty he began cleaning the weapon, swabbing and oiling and polishing until it shone like dark silver. One by one he cleaned the cartridges as meticulously as he had cleaned the rifle. Then he reloaded.

"The way you work on that rifle," a voice said, "a-body would guess you had some important work to put it to."

Gault looked up and quietly studied the man who was watching him through the open doorway. He was young—in his mid-twenties, Gault guessed. He was well rigged-out in California pants, gray flannel shirt and a pony hide vest. A nickel-plated star was fixed to the left side of the vest. So this, Gault reasoned, had to be Dub Finley, Standard County's one and only full-time deputy sheriff. "Did Olsen send you to keep an eye on me?"

Deputy Finley scowled. "Why would Sheriff Olsen want me to do that?" Gault noticed that Finley's thick black hair, which grew low on his forehead, formed a V between his eyes when he scowled. The eyes themselves were dark and wet-looking and without expression.

"I don't know," Gault said mildly. He gave the Winchester's breach a few wipes and put the rifle away. "What do you want?"

"I've had complaints about the pistol you're wearin'. New Boston ain't one of your rowdy trail towns, in case you landed here with that mistaken notion in your head. We're civilized. We got subscription schools, circuit courts, Methodist church, just like towns back East. Folks hereabouts don't feel called on to carry guns."

Gault heard the deputy's spiel out with a certain fascination. "All right," he said obligingly, "I'll take off the .45 and leave it with the hostler until I'm ready to leave."

"When will that be?"

"Hard to say right now. It depends."

Something crossed the deputy's mind and he frowned again. "You just mentioned the sheriff's name. Are you some kind of pal of Grady Olsen's?"

"No," Gault said with a thin smile. "I don't think you could rightly say that."

Finley worried this for a moment and then decided to take it up later with Olsen. He stepped up to the door of the shack and held out his hand. "I'll take that .45 now and leave it with the sheriff."

"I said I'd leave it with the hostler."

"That won't do." The deputy shook his head, and his hairline formed a black arrowhead that pointed straight down his narrow nose.

Gault hesitated for a moment, making no move to remove his cartridge belt. Still, there didn't seem to be much sense in making trouble for himself over the revolver. Like most plainsmen, he had never had much faith in hand guns anyway. He unbuckled the belt and handed the holstered weapon to Finley.

The deputy took it with a cool smile that seemed to imply

that he had won some sort of victory. With a curt little nod, he tucked the holstered Colt under his arm and strode away.

The shadows in front of the camp shacks were growing longer and darker. The day was dragging to a close and Gault could sense that the excitement of the day was beginning to pall. The funeral was over if not forgotten. The newspaper reporters, for the most part, had taken the noon stage out of New Boston. Visiting cowmen and farmers were beginning to straggle off in various directions.

It would be a day to remember, for most of them. The day they buried Wolf Garnett. For Frank Gault the day hadn't rightly started yet.

He went to the barn and left his rifle on the rack with his saddle. "I may want to rent a horse later," he told the hostler.

The rawhide little liveryman grinned and nodded his head. "That's what we're in business for." He squinted out at the dusty street. "Crowd's beginnin' to thin out some. I got an end shack now, closer to the pump, if you'd like to make a change."

He was afraid that a good-paying cash customer might move to the more convenient hotel. But it didn't matter to Gault where he stayed or how he lived. A man with a hot coal in his gut doesn't complain about a lumpy mattress. "Whereabouts is the graveyard from here?" he asked suddenly.

"You mean where they planted Wolf Garnett? Off to the north, on the slope there, maybe quarter of a mile. You can see it from the back of the barn."

As Gault was walking out of the barn the hostler called, "There's a smart little buckskin in the rent corral. I can put him back for you, if you want."

Gault hesitated, his gaze resting on a long-handled shovel in one of the feed stalls. "Maybe," he said, "you better do that."

CHAPTER TWO

The night was unseasonably cold for April; the sky glittered with ice-blue stars. Gault put the buckskin up the rocky slope to the north of New Boston. He reined up as he neared the cemetery and sat quietly until he was sure that he was not being followed. For perhaps the thousandth time he reminded himself that it wasn't too late to turn back. There was no doubt now that the dead man was Wolf Garnett; even his sister had identified him. The man he had seen in the Nations had been someone else.

Leave it alone, he told himself. Just go away from here and leave it alone.

He couldn't do it. His anger was too hot, the gall too bitter, the days too empty.

He nudged the buckskin and the cautious little animal began picking its way through the maze of earthen mounds. Gault had no trouble locating the newest grave. The mound was taller than the others, the earth around it scraped raw. There was no marker, no flowers, nothing at all to indicate that beneath that mound of clay lay a man who had once been feared all over Texas.

Slowly, Gault dismounted and staked the buckskin. He took the wagon yard shovel and plunged it into the mound.

It had been a dry winter; the shovel rang as it clashed with the flinty lumps of clay. The work went slowly, but it went steadily, and Gault developed a kind of grim rhythm with the shovel as he cleared away the mound and began work in the cavity of the grave itself.

The work went on and on, and there seemed to be no end to the length and breadth and depth of that dark grave. He worked until his muscles quivered, until rivers of sweat flowed down his face and dripped from the point of his chin, until his shirt was soaked and even his canvas windbreaker was wet. At last he had to stop. He fell against the side of the grave and gasped for breath. And for the first time he looked around him and saw himself standing there, almost shoulder deep in the new grave, and for the first time the question asked itself: *Lord, what am I doing!*

For one grim moment he thought that he would be sick. He closed his eyes and dragged great gulps of air into his burning lungs. Cold, moist air, smelling of the night and of the grave.

"Feelin' a little sick in your gut, are you, Gault?"

The big voice rolled and boomed with righteous indignation. Startled, Gault fell over his shovel and went to his knees. He wasn't sure whether he had actually heard the voice, or if it had been in his mind. He tilted his head and looked up from the depth of the grave, looked up at the huge figure of Grady Olsen looming against the star-scattered sky.

"Looks like you just ain't goin' to be satisfied any other way." The big sheriff's voice was slightly muffled now, sounding almost as if his jaws had been wired together. "All right, if that's what it takes to please you. Pick up your shovel. Dig."

Using the shovel as a support, Gault pulled himself to his feet. "Sheriff . . ." His mind was numb. He didn't know what it was that he wanted to say.

"Dig!" Olsen said again, this time with harshness and anger.

Almost without his willing it, Gault took the shovel in his hands and plunged it into the red clay. He lifted the shovel slowly while staring up at Olsen's wide, angry face, and dumped the few red clods over his shoulder. Only now did Gault notice the ugly twin muzzles of the sheriff's shotgun. As he dug, lifted, dumped the clay, the muzzles followed him like empty eyes.

Time dragged by. An hour. An eternity. "Careful," Olsen said finally. "You're about deep enough."

Gault had expected the solid feel of wood. But the dead man had been buried at county expense, and Standard County did not believe in squandering money on coffins.

"There," Olsen said at last. It was an angry sound.

The body had been sewn into a piece of castoff tarpaulin. Gault cast a curious glance at the sheriff. "You collected a thousand dollars in bounty. Would it have killed you to put him away in a pine box?"

"No time for that," the sheriff said impatiently. "Slit the tarp and look. Satisfy yourself once and for all. I don't want to have to go through this again."

Gault stood rigid, the shovel in his hands. He couldn't seem to make himself move.

"Have you got a knife?" Olsen asked.

Gault nodded. He felt in his pocket, took out a barlow pocketknife and opened it. For a moment the sheriff disappeared, then he appeared again, cast up against the dark sky. He had a lighted coal oil lantern in his hand. "All right, slit the tarp."

Again Gault's hand moved almost of its own will. He opened a two-foot slash in the tarpaulin. Grady Olsen got down on his knees and lowered the lantern into the grave.

Gault stared down at the horror at his feet. There was nothing there, nothing recognizable as a man.

"Gault, you all right?"

Gault could only stare at the horror. Two weeks in the water. He should have known. "Here," Olsen said. He pulled the lantern out of the grave. "Give me your hand."

Dumbly, Gault lifted his hand and the big sheriff hauled him out of the pit. Gault sat on the clay mound at the edge of the grave. "Are you satisfied now?" the sheriff asked.

He nodded wearily. The sheriff blew out the lantern. "Get your horse, we'll go back to town. I'll send somebody to fill the grave." When Gault didn't move, Olsen nudged him with the shotgun and his voice became harsh. "Nobody made you come up here and dig. And nobody told you it was goin' to be pretty."

With some effort, Gault pushed himself to his feet. The sheriff asked, "Are you convinced now?"

"Convinced of what?"

"That the dead man is Wolf Garnett?"

"I don't know," Gault said woodenly. "How can you tell?"

*

They rode the long grade down from the graveyard and reined up in the almost deserted street. "Now," Gault said indifferently, "you've got your duty to do, I guess."

"What duty is that?"

Gault lifted his head and studied the big sheriff for a moment. "From the way you talked up there, I figgered you just couldn't wait to get me to town where you could arrest me for grave-robbing."

The sheriff's smile was stiff and hostile. "That depends on what kind of plans you got. How long you figger to stay with us in New Boston?"

"It would be fine with me if I could leave on the next stage north."

"That won't be till day after tomorrow. You figger you can stay out of trouble till then?"

Gault allowed himself a taut smile. "I intend to work at it, Sheriff." The two men gazed at each other quietly. There didn't seem to be anything else to say, and finally Gault, with a little nod, reined away and rode toward the wagon yard.

So this, he thought emptily, is the way it ends. After almost a year of fury and grief, his only satisfaction was a grave on a barren hillside, a horror that had once been a man.

But had it been Wolf Garnett?

The hostler was not to be found, so Gault stripped the buckskin and turned the animal back into the rent corral. He went to his shack and methodically removed his boots and pants and shirt and stretched out on the rope-strung bunk. It would only be a matter of minutes, he knew, before armies of bedbugs began their inevitable attack—and he was not disappointed.

But not even the swarming insects could hold back those months of blackness that haunted him. When he closed his eyes Martha's face was there before him as he had last seen it, her eyes wide, glittering with terror. A few seconds later the stage had plunged off the mountain road. Gault had not seen his wife alive again.

MARTHA HENDERSON GAULT, BELOVED WIFE OF FRANKLIN KEARNY GAULT, BORN SEPTEMBER 4, 1864, DIED MARCH 12, 1885, REST IN PEACE.

Rest in peace, Gault thought darkly as the night wore on, for I cannot. A body in an unmarked grave was not enough—he had lost too much to have the debt balanced out so easily.

Before morning came he had made up his mind not to wait for the Thursday stage out of New Boston. At first light of a new day he got his meager gear together and found the hostler.

"Get the buckskin saddled. I'll be pullin' out directly after breakfast."

"If you aim to take the animal out every day you'd do better rentin' by the week."

"I'm not lookin' to rent. If the price is right, I'll buy." He walked off, giving the hostler a chance to settle on a price that would be at least half again what the buckskin was worth—but many months had gone by since Gault had given any thought to practicalities of business.

In the half light of the prairie dawn there was already one eating house open for business. NEW BOSTON RITZ CAFE, announced the sign on the flyspecked window, CHILI 10¢. Gault walked into a classic Southwest eating house. Six stools at an oilcloth-covered counter. Behind the counter there was an oldtime cowhand, too stove up to ride, who had decided in his later years to take up the art of cooking. The air was hot and heavy with grease.

The cook sidled up the counter, eying Gault narrowly. It was a trait of the New Boston citizen, Gault had noticed, to view any and all strangers with suspicion. "Ain't got the biscuits in yet," the cook announced sourly. "Want some coffee while you wait?"

Gault nodded. "Coffee. And never mind the biscuits. Bring me some flapjacks, three eggs and some bacon."

"Eggs come a dime apiece," the counterman said, as if he had serious doubts as to Gault's ability to pay for them.

"I'll take three," Gault insisted flatly. Then, as the only customer in the New Boston Ritz, he took an end stool and prepared to wait. The cook accepted the order grudgingly and sidled back to his grease-burning stove at the end of the counter. In his younger days, Gault guessed, the Ritz restaurateur had been a bronc buster. He had stayed with the job too long, too many rough rides had shaken his insides loose, which explained his bad disposition and his crablike movements behind the counter.

Gault was adding sugar and stirring his black, gritty

coffee, when the figure of Grady Olsen loomed like a thunderhead in the cafe doorway.

"The usual, Andy," Olsen called to the counterman. He took a stool next to Gault and said absently, "The wagon yard man says you're buyin' one of his rent animals. That mean you'll be pullin' out of New Boston ahead of the stage?"

"You get yourself up at first light just to ask the wagon yard man what I was up to?"

"Guess maybe I did, at that," Olsen admitted. "After all, you got some mighty queer habits, mister. It ain't every day we get grave-robbers in New Boston."

"You thinkin' about changin' your mind about arrestin' me?"

The sheriff chuckled quietly, adding canned milk and sugar to his coffee. "I ain't changed my mind, long's you behave yourself. But I couldn't help wonderin' why you're in such a big hurry to leave this little town of ours."

"I thought you wanted me to leave."

"And you thought right." The sheriff nodded and noisily sipped his coffee. "But when a man buys a rent horse from a wagon hostler, knowin' he's goin' to get skinned, just to save a few hours' time, well, it strikes me a mite queer. It strikes me you've got mighty little respect for cash money, or you're in a mighty big hurry to get out of New Boston. Am I barkin' up the right tree, Gault, or ain't I?"

The counterman brought Gault's order, slammed it down in front of him and gimped back to his stove. Gault gazed learily at the leathery flapjacks, the watery sugar syrup, the slabs of fat side meat, the puddles of grease already congealing in the cold platter. The eggs, also coated in congealing grease, were cooked to a peculiar bluish color, the whites curled, as if in pain, the yolks as hard as grape-shot. Gault cut into the flapjacks and began to eat. "No," he told the sheriff, "you're barkin' up the right tree. I'm ready enough to leave New Boston."

The sheriff sighed. It might have been a sigh of resignation, or it could have been in anticipation of a hearty breakfast. He folded his heavy arms across his chest and waited patiently until his meal arrived. "Andy's the best cook in Standard County," he said, taking up his knife and fork. He dug into his platter of hardcooked eggs and side meat and sour dough biscuits. "Where you aimin' to go?" he asked after the first rush of eating had taken the edge off his appetite.

"I don't know. Back to the Nations, maybe."

"Goin' back to runnin' cattle?"

". . . Maybe. I haven't thought much about it since . . ."

"Best forget about that," the sheriff said with as much gentleness as his big voice would allow. "It's a bitter dose to swaller, I reckon, but there's nothin' to be done about it now."

For the first time since their meeting, the sheriff seemed to warm to Gault and talk to him almost as a friend. Gault wondered why. Simply because he had decided to get out of New Boston? Could it really be that important?

Then something occurred to Gault. "Sheriff, about the two pals of Wolf Garnett's, that you mentioned yesterday. The ones that helped identify the body? Where are they now?"

Crady Olsen paused in his eating. Suddenly he wasn't so warm and friendly. "They ain't here. They was over in Sancho County takin' a herd up the Western Trail when they heard that Wolf's body'd been found. So they decided to ride over and have a look and make sure it was actual their old pard. It was."

"Did Wolf Garnett have many old pals like that? Good, law-abidin' gents, I take it, that would make a two day trip cross country just to look at his corpse?"

The sheriff's gray eyes became distant and cold.

Gault said, "It strikes me queer that a lobo like Garnett

would have friends that would go to so much trouble to help out the law."

The sheriff mopped up some cold grease with a biscuit and put it in his mouth. "Gault," he said wearily, "are you goin' to give me more trouble?"

"No, but I'd like to talk to those helpful pals of Garnett's."

"Can't be done," Olsen told him with feeling. "They went back to the herd. Must be halfway to Kansas by this time."

"What herd was it?"

". . . I don't recollect."

"What were the men's names?"

Olsen speared his last piece of side meat and chewed thoughtfully. "Colly Fay," he said reluctantly. "And Shorty Pike. The Fays and the Pikes used to farm on the Little Wichita, but they moved over to Sancho County a few years back. They was boys together with Wolf Garnett."

"When was that?"

"Five, six years ago."

"A long time," Gault said dryly. "They must have might good memories to be able to identify that body as Wolf Garnett."

The sheriff made a sound under his breath. It might have been a sigh, or a curse. "There was some talk of Colly and Shorty runnin' with Wolf's bunch, up till a year ago. Since that time they've been workin' at honest jobs. I can see what you're thinkin', but there was never any proof that the boys went outlawin' with Wolf. Just talk. Anyhow, the Pikes and the Fays are good, hardworkin' families, and I don't aim to bring them any trouble."

There was another question in Gault's mind, but he decided not to ask it now. He counted out some silver and left it beside his plate. "You pullin' out?" the sheriff asked.

"If the hostler doesn't hold me up over the buckskin."

"Remember what I told you. It's a sorry business about your wife, but let it drop. Best thing all around, for everybody."

Gault's smile was the strained expression of a man who hadn't tried it in a long while. "I'll think about it." He shoved himself away from the counter and walked out of the eating house.

*

Gault inspected the buckskin with an experienced eye. The animal was too small for his liking. Good enough to rent to women and children wanting to go out for a leisurely Sunday canter, but too light and spindle-legged for the kind of cross country travel that Gault had in mind. Still, the hoofs were in good shape and the shoes had been expertly fitted. All in all, Gault judged a fair price to be eighty dollars.

The hostler wanted two hundred. Gault pointed out the fragile forelegs and shallow barrel. The hostler cut his figure by twenty dollars and promised to throw in a Navajo saddle pad. Gault raised his figure to one hundred and twenty. The hostler said he'd throw in some camp gear and a bed that had been left by a bankrupt freighter. They settled on one hundred and forty dollars, and the hostler was to throw in the extra gear.

The wagon yard man took his money with little pleasure. Horse trading, to those who practiced it, was much more than simply a way of making a living—it was an art, and this kind of slack bargaining tended to cast the profession in a shoddy light.

"I guess you've lived in these parts a pretty good spell," Gault said casually, as he threw on the saddle and cinched it down.

The hostler looked at him suspiciously. "Long enough, I reckon."

Gault tied on the bedroll and slipped his Winchester in the saddle boot. "Then I guess you know where the Garnett place is."

The hostler lowered his gaze and began sliding away. "Can't say as I do. I got a poor memory for places. Especially places that ain't none of my business." He pocketed his money and walked off.

Gault jammed a knee in the buckskin's ribs and jerked the cinch down another notch when the startled animal sucked in its gut. With a final curious glance at the retreating hostler, Gault stepped into the stirrup and swung up to the saddle. He reined back toward the feed store where Sheriff Grady Olsen had his office.

The sheriff met him at the doorway. "I see you got the buckskin all right. That mean you'll soon be pullin' out of our fair city?"

"As soon as I get my .45."

"That's right," Olsen smiled blandly. "You gave your Colt to my deputy, didn't you?"

"He took it."

The sheriff scratched the stubble on his heavy jaw and assumed a puzzled expression. "Why would he want to do that?"

Gault experienced a flash of intuition that pointed the way this conversation was going to take. "Because you told him to take it," he said coldly. "Anyhow, that's what he said."

"Queer," Olsen said with a note of wonder. "I never told him to *take* the gun. Just to ask you to take it off. Must of been some kind of misunderstandin'." He spread his hands apologetically. "Well, we'll get to the bottom of it when Dub gets back."

Gault sensed that it was very unlikely that he would ever see that pistol again. With rising anger he asked, "Where is your deputy now?"

"Down in the south end of the county seein' about a case of brand splotchin'. I expect him back in three, four days. If he don't run into trouble."

"I don't care about the deputy, just give me the Colt."

The big lawman assumed an elaborate air of innocence and Gault decided that Grady Olsen had missed his calling. He was a born actor. "I'd be proud to hand over your pistol, Gault, if I knowed where it was. But I'm scared we'll have to wait and ask Dub Finley about that."

That was the way it was going to be. Gault was packed and eager to get away from New Boston, and Olsen knew it.

The sheriff had rightly guessed that Gault would not postpone leaving for another three or four days because of a single Colt revolver.

"Wish I could be more help," the lawman said blithely. "If you don't want to wait, I reckon I could express the gun to you. If you tell me where you want it sent."

Gault gazed at that wide open face and honest eyes and wondered why a respected county sheriff would lie and cheat and connive, all because of one inexpensive hand gun. As he thought about it his early anger began to settle. Curiosity, and a kind of vague unease, took its place. "Never mind," he said dryly. "Might be I'll be passin' through here again sometime." He turned on his heel and went down the outside stairway.

He climbed up to the saddle and sat there for a moment before reining away from the rack. The sheriff was looking down at him, his big face blank, his hands grasping the railing of the second-floor gallery. *What's he up to?* The question rolled in Gault's mind but found no satisfactory answer. For a moment he was tempted to dismount and buy another revolver—but he had the uneasy feeling that New Boston stores would be out of revolvers that day. Gault turned a last curious glance up at Grady Olsen.

With the innocence of angels, the sheriff smiled down at him. Gault hauled the buckskin away from the rack and pointed the animal up the main street of New Boston, heading north.

Was it his imagination, or did the town actually seem to

hold its breath for a moment? A prickling sensation scurried across Gault's scalp. He had the feeling that from behind every window along the street a pair of eyes was watching him.

The hostler was standing in front of the livery barn, arms folded across his chest, his eyes fixed on Gault. Gault nodded as he rode past. The hostler turned abruptly and walked into the barn.

When he had put the town behind him and it was no longer in sight, Gault reined off the Gainsville mail road and struck northwest toward the Little Wichita. He had been out of New Boston for a little more than an hour when a disquieting thought came to him. He jerked the Winchester out of the saddle boot and began inspecting it.

It took only a few seconds to discover that the firing pin had been neatly filed away. When or by whom he couldn't say, but he guessed it to be the work of the hostler, or possibly Deputy Dub Finley. Probably while Gault had been digging in the New Boston graveyard.

Not that any of those things mattered now. The thing that mattered was that someone, for reasons of his own, had very quietly and efficiently disarmed him.

CHAPTER THREE

It was a pleasant spring day in North Texas. The rolling prairie was sparkling green, the sky a dazzling blue. Cattle, fat and sleek, lazed in the new grass. Along the streams budding cottonwoods and oaks were coming into leaf. The sun was warm, the air so clean that it tasted faintly of flint and steel. All in all, it was a near perfect day for travelers.

Frank Gault did not enjoy it. He was not even aware of the calm beauty that surrounded him.

For the past hour he had suspected that he was being followed; within the past few minutes he had become certain of it. There were two of them at least, maybe three. They lay far back on his backtrail, popping up from behind ridges and knolls, moving when Gault moved, stopping when he stopped. Usually there was only one of them in sight at a time, and never more than two.

Near midafternoon Gault dismounted at a small stream and let the buckskin drink and graze for several minutes. Far to the south, appearing as little more than a speck on the horizon, one of the riders topped a rise and stopped. Could it be the sheriff? Gault didn't think so. Even at that distance, Gault was sure that he would recognize Grady Olsen's slope-shouldered figure if he were to see it.

The deputy, maybe? Gault had met the deputy only

once, and the young lawman had not greatly impressed him. It was impossible to tell at that distance.

Whoever they were, they seemed to be playing a waiting game. Waiting and watching. Gault would have given a great deal to know why.

He rebalanced and tied the bulky bedroll behind the saddle and once again pointed the buckskin toward the northwest. The horsebacker on the far horizon moved casually across the green prairie and disappeared in a stand of blackjack. In a few minutes one of the other riders appeared on a wooded knoll, maybe a mile to the east of the first one.

Gault began to experience an ill-defined ache in his gut. At first it occurred to him that the surly proprietor of the New Boston Ritz had poisoned him. Then he recognized it for what it was—a subtle but steadily growing fear. It was not an unfamiliar experience—all cattlemen knew it well. A horse going off a cut bank on a dark night. The suck of quicksand. Stumbling in front of a stampede.

But this was different. It was a quiet but growing thing. The kind of sensation that went with the knowledge that he was unarmed and helpless in a hostile country.

Late that afternoon Gault reached the Little Wichita and prepared to make camp in a grove of rattling cottonwoods. The distant horsebackers were not to be seen, but he had no doubt that they were there. Waiting and watching.

The prairie sun took a long time dying. Gault staked the buckskin in new grass and built his fire. He did not bother to make it small or smokeless—the watchers would see it, however small he made it. Methodically, he inspected the meager camp gear that the hostler had thrown in with the buckskin. A small skillet, a granite coffeepot, a spoon, all wrapped in a faded tarpaulin and a dirty patchwork quilt. In his own warbag he had a small parcel of cornmeal, a piece of dry salt meat and some crushed coffee beans.

He cut off a slab of salt meat and put it in the skillet to cook. He dipped some water into the coffeepot, added the crushed beans and set it beside the skillet. From far upstream he heard the faint rustle of brush. It might have been a deer. Or a wild turkey settling on a cottonwood branch for the night. But he didn't think so.

Gault smiled thinly to himself as the smell of cooking meat spread on the still air. He wondered if the watchers would dare to build fires, or if they would lay back cautiously and make do with cold trail fare that night.

The shadows along the river became longer and blacker. Night, with its hundreds of fluttering and scurrying sounds, came to the Little Wichita. The darkness of springtime was chill and damp, but no fires appeared on the prairie. It was small satisfaction knowing that his watchers were hungry and cold—but it was better than no satisfaction at all.

Gault stirred cornmeal and water into the meat grease and cooked the panbread over glowing embers. He ate in silence, without relish or satisfaction, and then he washed the skillet with sand and water and put it away.

They must know I'm unarmed, he reasoned to himself. If they wanted to finish me off they could have done it any time. Still, they're not going to all this trouble on a mere whim.

They were waiting to see what his next move would be. Now that he had reached the Little Wichita, would he cross the stream and head due north toward the Nations, or would he bear to the east and scout the river valley, looking for the Garnett farm?

If he made for the Nations, that would indicate that he had convinced himself that the body in the grave was actually that of Wolf Garnett and that any further investigation was useless. In which case, Gault speculated, the riders would trail him as far as the Red to satisfy themselves that he was actually making for the Nations. Then they would go back to wherever it was they came from.

On the other hand, if he struck up the valley of the Little Wichita looking for Wolf Garnett's homeplace, the watchers would likely regard it as a suspicious move.

And then what? The watchers—or someone—had managed to disarm him. Would they go as far as killing him? It didn't seem reasonable—but he was learning that the world wasn't necessarily a reasonable place. The cold-blooded act of whipping a stage team off a mountain road hadn't been reasonable. But it had happened.

When the fire had burned down Gault threw his bed near a gnarled elm. He lay quietly, gazing blindly through the twisted branches. Was it possible that the men who were following him had been with Wolf Garnett that day?

For the thousandth time he saw the frightened horses racing off into thin air, and the coach turning slowly, end over end, before crashing on the rocks below.

He sat up suddenly in a cold sweat. I've got to stop this, he thought grimly. Pretty soon I'll be keening like a Comanche squaw and slashing my arms with knives. He dug into his windbreaker for makings and built a smoke. The sulphur match flared like a muzzle flash when he lit the cigarette.

He looked back at the dark trees along the river. Not since sundown had there been any sign of the men who were watching him. But they were there. He had no doubt of that. How long do you aim to sit out there, he thought bleakly, without hot grub, without even a smoke?

Gault snapped his own smoke toward the dying embers. To hell with you, he told them silently. Sooner or later I'll find out who you are. But for right now, to hell with you. He closed his eyes and made a desert of his mind. An April dew settled on his bed with clammy coldness, but he ignored it. He drifted into a state of dreamlessness that passed as sleep. The watchers, wherever they were, remained silent and invisible.

*

The morning was chill and damp and heady with the smell of green things growing. Gault stirred himself before first light and rebuilt the fire and put coffee on to boil. He saw to the buckskin and then scouted the upper banks for tracks. But the watchers of the night had kept their distance.

From somewhere upstream a wild bird beat the air with its wings. The watchers were moving in closer, and they were not being so quiet about it now. Gault gulped his gritty coffee and chewed on leftover panbread that he had cooked the night before.

He got the buckskin saddled, then rolled his bed and made it fast behind the cantle. He slid the Winchester into the saddle boot without bothering to check it, as he normally would. If his trackers were watching, maybe they would think that he hadn't yet discovered the ruined firing pin.

Gault climbed up to the saddle. All right, boys, he thought quietly, from here on out you better keep a close watch. Because I ain't right sure myself which way I'm going to take.

A short distance downstream he put the buckskin over a rock crossing that Comanches and Kiowas had probably used not many years before when they were raiding down from the Territory. Due north was the Big Pasture and the Nations, where Frank Gault was known and respected. Where there were men who would lend him money to get started again, if he were to ask for it.

But he did not head north. He bore east, making for the upper reaches of the Little Wichita. And behind him he could almost hear his trailers shrug resignedly and check the loading of their weapons.

Around midmorning Gault caught a glimpse of the lead rider. He was a short, blocky man with a blunt, pugnacious look about him. Expertly, he threaded a sturdy little clay-bank in and out through the stands of cottonwood and oak. They were moving in fast now, not overly concerned with whether or not Gault spotted them.

A few minutes later Gault raised the fields that he guessed belonged to the Garnetts. There were several acres of cotton in even rows, almost ready for its first thinning and chopping. Set farther back from the river there was a good-sized patch of early corn, young and tender green and languid looking on that mild spring morning. Closer to the house and sheds was what Gault knew to be a vegetable garden, although he couldn't tell at that distance what was planted there.

The house itself was a half sod, half timber affair, maybe three rooms. A big house, Gault thought immediately; an unusually prosperous looking spread for that particular part of Texas. The rare farm that Gault had chanced across in North Texas usually amounted to no more than a one-room soddy and maybe two or three acres of scratched red clay. The Garnett place included several permanent sheds and outbuildings, some work animals, a wagon, a scattering of chickens and probably a cow for milking. A *very* prosperous looking layout, Gault thought again with bitterness. Either the Garnetts were exceptionally industrious, or they had received considerable help.

A rider that Gault had not seen before appeared from a wild plum thicket near the water. He was a stolid, slack-jawed man in his middle years, with coarse features and the impersonal stare of simple-mindedness in his pale eyes. He rode toward Gault with an abstracted grin tugging at the corners of his mouth—but there was nothing simple-minded or unbusinesslike in the way he held a short saddle rifle pointed at Gault's chest.

"Set easy," the man said placidly. "We don't aim to hurt you. If you behave yourself and mind what we say."

Gault twisted in the saddle and saw the short man coming toward them from a thicket farther upstream. When he was close enough to be heard, the short man said, "My advice is do like Colly tells you. He may not look right bright, but there ain't many men hereabouts that can best him with a rifle."

Colly. The name struck a spark in Gault's mind. He remembered the two pals of Wolf Garnett's that the sheriff had mentioned. One had been Colly Fay. The other Shorty Pike. Two harmless drovers working a herd up the Western Trail to Dodge, the sheriff had said. Two ignorant farm boys who had fallen in with bad company for a while. But they had seen the error of their ways and turned back to the path of honesty and truth—according to Sheriff Grady Olsen. Gault wondered if Sheriff Olsen would be surprised if he could have seen his two farm boys now, both of them with snub-barreled rifles pointed at Gault's chest.

Gault did not look at the rifles. He did his best to act and talk as if they were not there at all. "You boys strayed pretty far from bedground, looks like. Sheriff Olsen seemed to figger you'd gone back to drivin' cattle, after you took it on yourselves to ride over to New Boston and identify Wolf Garnett's body."

Colly Fay continued to smile abstractedly. Shorty Pike shrugged his shoulders and casually slipped his saddle gun back in its boot. "We won't go into that now. Just say we changed our mind."

All right, Gault thought, let's see what kind of cards you're holding! He glanced toward the field of green corn and asked, "Is that the Garnett place?"

Shorty took a deep breath and made a quiet decision of his own. "That what you been lookin' for? The Garnett place?"

Gault made himself smile. "Just wonderin'. Curiosity, you might say."

The muzzle of Colly's rifle moved a fraction of an inch, as if hunting the exact center of Gault's chest. Shorty folded his hands on the saddle horn and looked at Gault and said nothing. Apparently the next move would come from another direction.

"Look," Gault said in a tone of extreme reasonableness, "I don't know why folks are so dead set against lettin' me talk to Wolf Garnett's sister. I don't aim to pester her or give her any more grief than she's already come in for. All I want is to talk to her about her brother."

"Why?"

"I want to satisfy myself that Wolf Garnett is dead."

Shorty glanced at his partner and smiled. He touched his forehead with his finger to suggest that Gault was more than a little loco. Colly Fay chuckled absently and nodded.

A third rider approached silently along Gault's backtrail. He swung down toward the river and came toward them through a grove of cottonwoods. Gault turned cautiously to look at him—and somehow he was not surprised when he saw that it was Standard County's only full-time deputy sheriff, Dub Finley.

Gault leaned forward on the saddle horn and said dryly, "I don't guess you boys rode all this way just to give me back my .45, did you?"

Finley shot a look at Shorty Pike, and the squarest little man said, "We never stopped him until we seen he was makin' straight for the farm."

The deputy frowned and his hairline pointed down the center of his forehead. "What are you after, Gault?"

What was he after? Gault had asked himself the question many times, and he still wasn't sure of the answer. Revenge? Satisfaction? Justice? He didn't know. He only knew that there was a wild thing inside that would not let him rest—and maybe, if he could be sure that Wolf Garnett was dead, the thing could be tamed and lived with. But all he said to the deputy was, "I want to ask Wolf's sister some questions."

"All the folks that count," the deputy said bluntly, "have already asked their questions. Representatives of the express company and the cattlemen's association, that had bounties on Wolf's head. County lawmen and U.S. marshals that had warrants for his arrest. Newspaper writers from all over. For almost three days Esther had questions throwed at her from ever' which way—almost more'n a woman could stand. It got her so upset she couldn't even come to New Boston for the funeral." Dub Finley wanted to be the cool, efficient and responsible lawman that he imagined himself to be, but he was by nature hotheaded and impulsive. In spite of himself, his voice was slowly rising up the scale of anger. "What I'm sayin', Gault, is she's had enough. She ain't goin' to be plagued with any more questions. Not while I'm deputy here."

"What does Sheriff Olsen say about it?"

Finley smiled unpleasantly. "Me and the sheriff see alike on this." Again he made an effort to rein himself in. "I'm sorry about what happened to your wife. But that was almost a year ago. And Wolf Garnett's dead. My advice is forget it, Gault."

Forget it. Pretend the sweaty nightmares weren't there. Pretend that Martha was still radiant and warm and that her murder had never happened. "Forgettin'," he said with a curious flatness, "ain't an easy thing to do."

"I guess," the young deputy said unfeelingly, "it's somethin' you'll have to learn." He brushed some trail dust from his pony hide vest. This reminded him how long he had been out trailing Gault, and how long it had been since he had had hot food or proper rest, and this realization whetted his pugnaciousness to a fine edge. "I don't aim to keep on tellin' you, Gault. This is the last time. Go on back to where you came from."

Somewhere in the back of Gault's mind the quiet voice of reasonableness said, "He's probably right. I'm not doing myself any good, carryin' on this way. It won't bring Martha back. And you can't go on hating a dead man all your life. If he is dead. And the experts claim he is. So it doesn't really make any difference whether or not you talk to Wolf Garnett's sister . . ."

But when he looked at the smug arrogance in the deputy's face, he said "Tell your gunhands to get out of my way. I aim to talk to Miss Garnett—unless you're willin' to go as far as to shoot me."

"I'll go as far as I need to," Dub Finley said, and Gault had no doubt that he meant it.

Even now the young deputy was quietly taking his measure. Gault could see it in those remote eyes. He was making up his mind whether he ought to kill him here and now, stopping all argument and saving himself a lot of trouble. Gault, in spite of the thing that drove him, was chilled at what he saw in Deputy Finley's eyes.

Colly Fay was gazing at Gault and grinning vacantly. Shorty Pike sat like a square stump, apparently waiting for some signal from Finley. Gault discovered that his mouth was suddenly dry. His tongue felt thick and furry. No one had bothered to remove his rifle from its saddle boot—they were confident that the weapon was useless and that he was helpless. The only problem of the moment seemed to be whether or not he was worth shooting.

A fine bead of sweat began to form on Gault's forehead. Somehow he had never expected things to go this far. But then, he reminded himself, a man used to living within the law is always surprised at the prospect of murder. It had surprised him once before.

He forced himself to sit quietly and tried not to stare at Colly Fay's saddle gun. Dub Finley looked at him with a cool little smile and shrugged his shoulders. The gesture said louder than words, "There's nothing for it, Gault. If I let you go, you'd only come back and cause trouble later. I might as well get it over with now."

Gault suddenly stared at an invisible point just beyond Colly Fay's shoulder. He stared with all the surprise and fascination that he could muster. Colly blinked, as Gault had hoped he would. The simple-minded rifleman scowled and half-turned in his saddle to see what it was behind him that was so completely fascinating. For an instant the muzzle of the rifle was pulled off line with Gault's chest. Gault struck at it savagely. The weapon fell from Colly's surprised hands, and Gault heard it thud quietly to the soft turf.

By that time Gault had jerked the startled buckskin around and was spurring toward the covering timber along the river. Even while he was doing it he was thinking, there's no use. Finley's already made up his mind and he will never let me get as far as the river.

He was right. Almost immediately a second rifle, this one belonging to Shorty Pike, spoke bitingly in the clean morning air. Gault felt the bee sting on his left side. Almost instantly the bee sting was a rapidly spreading numbness—and, in dizzying sequence, the numbness became a dazzling center of pain.

He thought angrily to himself: It's nothing. No more than a glancing hit at worse. Maybe a cracked rib. Nothing more than that.

But already he was falling. There was no more shooting. That was a bad sign, for it meant that Shorty himself must be convinced that he was done for. Gault grabbed for the saddle horn and missed. He continued to fall with nightmarish slowness. He remembered trying, without success, to shake his foot free of the stirrup. Then the ground loomed up and struck him with hammerlike force. The buckskin dragged him for another hundred yards before his foot came free—but Gault did not remember that.

*

After what seemed a very long time but could not have been more than a few minutes, Gault became aware of an almost endless expanse of startlingly blue sky. He lay on his back against a stone outcrop that had eventually stopped his rolling and tumbling. There was fire in his side and no air in his lungs. Fighting for breath, he tried to push himself erect. The toe of a dusty boot planted itself in his chest and pushed him back on the damp earth.

Deputy Dub Finley moved in to stand up against the shimmering backdrop of blue sky. From Gault's position, he looked as tall as a mountain. He had drawn his .45 and was holding it in his right hand, thoughtfully tapping the muzzle in the palm of his left hand while he gazed unblinkingly down at Gault.

As if from a great distance, Gault heard Shorty Pike say, "Somebody comin'."

Then the picture became confused. The sky turned dark. The figure of Deputy Finley loomed huge and tilted at a sickening angle. Gault closed his eyes in an effort to keep the sky from spinning. From a void he heard voices and echoes of voices. Some were angry and excited. Others cool and dangerous. Gault didn't open his eyes to see where the voices were coming from. At the moment it didn't seem to matter. In spite of his efforts, the world began to spin. Darkness came down on him like the lid of a coffin.

CHAPTER FOUR

"Here," a voice was saying, "you better take some of this."
It was a calm, no-nonsense feminine voice.

Gault heard the voice but did not respond to it. He let himself float, like an aimless raft on a sluggish river, in a shadow world that was neither sleep nor consciousness. After a while—he didn't know how long—the owner of the voice went away.

He drifted, without thinking or feeling. At last a shaft of dazzling light struck his eyes and shocked him awake. Squinting, he saw that he was on a bed of loose hay, in a small building that seemed to be a shed of some kind—a feed shed or a small barn. There was a half loft above, and two pole cubicles below which might have been feeding or milking stalls. The light that had shocked him awake was a slant of sunlight coming through the poorly chinked wall.

Gault rolled over on the mound of hay, to get the sun out of his eyes, and was immediately sorry for his rashness. An arrow of pain pierced his left side and pinned him to the ground. He was still gasping for breath when a shadow fell across the floor of the shed, and the no-nonsense voice asked, "Do you feel like eatin' now?"

For several seconds Gault could only stare at her. She

moved toward him and stood over him, looking down at him. "Best not move around too sharp," she told him unnecessarily. "There ain't much wrong with you, but might a busted rib where the bullet shied off."

She said it as though someone got shot every day or so around the place, and it was nothing to get excited about. She pulled up a three-legged milking stool and sat down and looked at him steadily. "What's the matter with you? Can't you talk?"

"I can talk," Gault said with some bitterness. "It's the breathin' that bothers me."

"That's on account of the bindin' sheet I tied around you. I seen old Doc Doolie do it once to a hand that fell off a horse and busted some ribs."

"How long have I been here?"

"Two, three hours, all told. Took some time to haul you over here after Shorty shot you. Fool thing for him to do, and I told him so."

Gault stared at her. Two surprisingly clear eyes peered at him from beneath the hood of her sunbonnet—that was about all he could see of her face. Besides the sunbonnet, she wore the long, shapeless gray gingham dress that all farm women seemed to favor. In the country west of Kansas City there must have been a thousand farm wives just like her, looking almost as if they had been cut from the same pattern. And yet, there was something about this woman. The bluntness and briskness of youth, Gault guessed it was.

"I reckon you better lay back and rest a spell," she said, after a few moments' consideration. "Ain't good to get yourself stirred up after bein' shot. That's what my ma always said."

"Shorty Pike," Gault said, trying to keep his voice even. "And the ones that were with him. Did you see which way they went?"

Those clear eyes beneath the sunbonnet hood blinked

at him. "They didn't go nowhere, they're over at my kitchen eatin' dinner." The woman stood up, nodded briskly and said, "I got some marrow bone broth on the stove. It'll perk you up some."

"Ma'am," Gault said as she made for the shed door, "just to get somethin' clear in my mind . . . Are you Wolf Garnett's sister?"

"Course I am," she said quietly. "Ever'body knows that."

Gault closed his eyes and made his mind a blank. The shaft of sunlight moved persistently across his bed of hay and fell once again across his face, but he was too bewildered to notice it, and too tired to move.

❋

Gault had been awake only a few minutes when he became aware of the tall figure darkening the doorway. Deputy Dub Finley came into the shed, his face scowling and thoughtful, his hairline pointing straight down the slender bridge of his nose. "You're a lucky man, Gault," he said quietly. "You ought to be a gambler. With your luck."

Gault looked at the deputy's dark countenance and decided that, unpleasant as it was, it was not the face of a man bent on immediate murder. "I guess," he said harshly, "there ain't much sense in askin' if you're goin' to arrest Shorty Pike for shootin' me."

"Arrest Shorty Pike?" The young lawman was amused. "We seen you clear as day, down in the riverbottom, fixin' to run off two of the Garnett milk cows. We hollered at you, and that's when you started shootin' at us. Shorty fired in self-defense. No two ways about it."

Gault forced himself to speak without shouting. "What did I use for a gun when I was doin' all this shootin'?"

"Why your Winchester, of course."

"Maybe you'd tell me how I could fire a rifle that didn't have a firing pin?"

The deputy grinned. "There ain't nothin' wrong with that rifle, Gault. I checked it myself. The firin' pin's good as new."

Gault had no doubt that it *was* new, but there was no way he could prove it. If he wanted to be stubborn and take the matter to court, it would be his word against Finley's. And he didn't have to guess which side the judge would believe. Still, it was a fact that the deputy had tried to kill him. *Would* have killed him, if Esther Garnett hadn't happened along when she had.

"See what I mean, Gault?" The deputy favored Gault with a one-sided smile. "Maybe next time Miss Garnett won't happen along in time to help you. Luck, they say, has a way of runnin' out."

"Finley," Gault said wearily, "would you tell me somethin'?"

"Be proud to," the deputy said dryly. "What is it you want to know?"

"The sheriff, what I saw of him, didn't strike me as a scalp hunter. What does he aim to do with the bounty money when he collects?"

This was not the question that Finley had expected, but he shrugged and answered without hesitation. "Why, he'll give it over to Miss Esther. What did you figger he'd do with it?"

Suddenly Gault was tired of the deputy and tired of talking. Finley hunkered down next to the straw bed, studying Gault with curiosity, as a small boy might have studied a horned toad sleeping in the sun. He felt for makings and meticulously built and lit a cigarette. "Like I say," he said mildly. "You been runnin' in luck. But a smart gambler knows when the cards're startin' to turn on him. What kind of a gambler are you, Gault?"

"A curious one."

Finley shook his head sadly. "The worst kind." He finished his smoke and shoved himself to his feet.

"I take it," Gault said acidly, "that you and the sheriff, and some others, don't want me in Standard County any longer. Might be I'd leave, and save you the trouble of killin' me, if I knowed why it was that you didn't want me here."

Finley smiled. It was a chilling expression on a humorless face. "Miss Esther ain't had much schoolin', but she's a tolerable good doc. She'll have you up and around inside of two, three days. Your buckskin's in the horse pen on the other side of the shed. My advice is get saddled soon as you're able to ride, and strike for some direction away from Standard County."

The deputy nodded and strode out of the shed. Gault lay for a long while, his mind milling in aimless circles. He saw Shorty Pike and Colly Fay pass in front of the open doorway, heading for the Garnett cornfield with long-handled hoes on their shoulders.

Gunhands hoeing corn. It made a bizarre picture. And it raised bizarre and disturbing thoughts in his mind.

He drifted into a troubled sleep, and when he awoke Esther Garnett was standing over him with a large crock bowl in her hands. "Deputy Finley said you was in a hurry to get well so's you could start back to your home-place. You won't be doin' much ridin' for three, four days. And not then, if you don't start eatin'." She pulled up the milking stool and sat down and handed him the bowl.

"Sorry to put you out," he said with lingering bitterness. "I didn't aim to go and get myself shot on your property."

She ignored his heavy sarcasm. "Wasn't your fault," she told him. "All a misunderstandin'. Deputy Finley and Shorty and Colly thought you was drivin' off my cows."

There didn't seem to be any point in arguing about it. Gault gazed down at the soup, a rich brown broth swimming with grease and chunks of marrow. The thought of eating any of it caused his stomach to curl. What he wanted was a large glass of whiskey and some rest. More than anything else, a night of dreamless sleep. A night of oblivion in which Martha's terrified eyes did not haunt him.

"Eat," Esther Garnett said briskly, those clear eyes watching him from beneath the hood of her sunbonnet.

Gault dipped a spoon through the layer of grease and took some of the broth in his mouth. It was as bad as he had feared. After a few spoonfuls he put the bowl aside.

"Come breakfast time," she told him, "you'll feel more like eatin'." Gault lay back on the hay. For some time those clear eyes continued to look at him from beneath the hood of the sunbonnet. Then, in a gesture of mild irritation, she shoved the sunbonnet back with her forearm and let it hang down her back.

The change was startling. At first Gault was struck by what appeared to be her extreme youth. Her oval face was as smooth and as delicately tinted as Dutch china. She's only a child! Gault thought in amazement. He saw almost immediately that this was a mistake—there was something childlike in the blue clearness of her eyes, and in the delicacy of her complexion—but she was no child. Gault wondered about her age and guessed it at eighteen. Almost immediately he revised it upward to twenty, and finally settled on twenty-four or -five.

It took him several minutes to find the right word to describe her, and it came as something of a surprise when he realized that the word was "beautiful." It had not occurred to him before that beauty was such a rare thing on the frontier. Martha had not been beautiful—she had been pleasing to look at, and he had loved her—but she had not been beautiful.

He realized that he was staring. But apparently Esther Garnett was used to being stared at. She smiled and picked up the bowl. "Deputy Finley said your name is Gault."

Gault nodded. The thing about her that fascinated him was the rosy tint of her skin. In the Southwest a woman's face tended to become dark and leathery. At the age of thirty she was an old woman. Mostly because of the heat and the wind. At forty they began losing their teeth, and often their hair. It had something to do with not getting enough of the right things to eat, Gault had heard. He wasn't sure about that, but he did know that Southwest summers were hell on women. Or on anything at all, for that matter, that was delicate and lovely to look at. Wild flowers that sometimes dotted the prairie lasted only a few days. And Gault was sure that Esther Garnett too would soon begin to fade. But for the moment she was beautiful.

*

That night a sudden thunderstorm rolled in from the west, and for an hour the night shuddered with thunder and lightning, and rain slashed into the shed through the poorly chinked walls. Gault was grateful for the storm, and while it lasted he remembered his trail-driving days, before he had had a brand of his own. Then his biggest worries had been being struck by lightning or having his horse stumble in front of a stampede. His worst nightmares had been simple ones, like riding off a cut bank on a stormy night. Not like the ones now.

The storm, like most prairie storms, did not last long. Gault propped himself up on the mound of hay. The freshly washed night smelled cold and clean. He could hear water running in some distant gully or arroyo. Somewhere a nervous horse—perhaps the buckskin—huffed and stamped.

The storm passed, but Gault was afraid to sleep. Afraid to dream. He built a cigarette and lit it and smoked it slowly. Maybe, he thought to himself, I'll go away from here. As soon as I feel like ridin'. Maybe I'll head back to the Big Pasture country and lease some grass from the Comanches and Kiowas and start running cattle again.

No, he corrected himself, almost immediately, not the Big Pasture. That would remind him of his time with

Martha. Maybe some state land, over in the Panhandle. There was still some open range left, in spite of the encroaching sodbusters and squatters.

He knew only too well that this was wishful thinking. There was a wild man locked up inside him. And rivers of bile. They would not let him rest or work or do any of the quietly productive things that ordinary men did.

He sat for a long while in the darkness of the shed. The last remnants of the storm had passed on to the east. An April moon and a few glittering stars looked coldly down on North Texas. Through the side cracks in the split pole walls, Gault looked bleakly out at the Garnett farmhouse and sheds. This, Gault thought, is where Wolf Garnett once lived. The outlaw had, no doubt, been in this very shed many times.

The taste of steel was in Gault's mouth. He tried to turn his thoughts in other directions. And for a little while he almost succeeded. He was about to get himself settled again and try to sleep when, suddenly, the flare of a sulphur match lighted up a small corner of the outside darkness. The deputy, Gault thought to himself. Or Pike, or Fay. They're still here.

Whoever it was, the light had come from a blacksmith lean-to next to the main barn, on the far side of the house. Gault waited for several minutes, scowling, but there were no more lights.

Gault was settling again on his hay bed when he first heard the sound of hoofs in the distance. Gingerly, he raised himself and peered through the crack. Apparently, he wasn't the only one to hear horses—a slender figure appeared out of the dark bulk of the barn and stood for a moment in the soft moonlight. He cocked his head to one side, listening. The man was too tall for Pike, and not big enough for Fay. It was Deputy Dub Finley, and, for some reason, he had been waiting there in the barn for just the sound that he was now hearing.

Gault's curiosity was whetted. He watched the deputy move a little farther out from the barn, his head still cocked, listening. Suddenly he began walking toward the approaching horsebackers, and after a few steps he broke into a jog. Soon the deputy had disappeared behind what was probably a small harness shed.

Gault started to pull himself to his feet in order to get a better look, but a pain went through him like a knife and he fell back gasping. He mopped the beads of cold sweat from his forehead and listened for the horsebackers.

There was no sound of hoofs. The night breathed quietly. In the far distance there was the faintest echo of thunder. The land lay as still and cold as a freshly washed corpse. Then, at last, the horses came on at a slow walk, making for the farmhouse, as near as Gault could tell. Cautiously, he returned to a sitting position and pressed his eye to the crack.

Two horses appeared beyond the building that Gault guessed to be the harness shed. Two riders got down, tied up at a corral and for several moments stood talking to Finley. One of the newcomers was a big, slope-shouldered man, heavy in his movements, and Gault recognized him immediately as the sheriff of Standard County, Grady Olsen. The other man was much smaller than Olsen and carried something vaguely round in shape, almost as large as a blanket roll, under one arm. Gault found this second figure slightly familiar but could not place him in his mind.

Leaving their horses, the three men made for the farmhouse in a roundabout way, keeping as much distance as possible between themselves and the shed where Gault was supposed to be sleeping. Gault lost sight of them as they entered the farmhouse. A faint light appeared in one of the farmhouse windows.

Long minutes dragged by. Gault could only guess at the time, but judging from the visible shift of the moon and stars, the three men had been inside the Garnett house for at least two hours. At the end of this time Gault sagged exhausted against the wall of the shed. For a time he tried to make some sense out of what had happened and what he had seen—but too many pieces of the puzzle were missing.

Standard County, he decided, was a puzzling place, and the most puzzling part of it was Sheriff Grady Olsen himself. Although the sheriff accepted scalp money and ran his county with an iron fist, he had been re-elected to office over and over. For his only deputy he had hired a cat-eyed assassin who, in turn, was aided by two gunhands who had once ridden with Wolf Garnett.

And Esther Garnett—where did she fit into the puzzle of Standard County? Why had Olsen and the second horse-backer braved a prairie storm, in the middle of the night, to talk to her? Wearily, Gault closed his eyes.

Exhaustion overtook him and for a time a restless sleep came down on him. When he awoke he noticed that the moon and stars had taken up radically new positions in the steely sky. He must have been asleep for an hour. Maybe longer.

The two horses, he noticed, were no longer tied at the distant corral. There was no movement in the farmyard. No light in the house.

*

After a time Gault had fallen asleep, but he slept fitfully and was awake again at first light. Esther Garnett appeared in the doorway with a plate of smoked side meat, hard-fried eggs and biscuits.

"Guess you heard the storm last night," she said briskly. "Blowed out one of my window lights in the kitchen."

Gault studied her closely in the harsh light. She was still as lovely and delicately tinted as Dutch china. "I heard some of it," he told her, "but mostly I slept."

Gault couldn't tell whether or not she believed him. "Here," she said, handing him the plate, "commence on this while I fetch you some coffee."

It was on the tip of Gault's tongue to ask about the two night visitors, but at the last moment he bit the question back. He dug half-heartedly into the meat and eggs.

Esther appeared again in the doorway, carrying a blackened coffeepot and a granite cup. "Can't expect a man to have his wits about him," she said, "until he's had his mornin' coffee. That's what my pa always said."

"Where's your pa now?" Gault asked curiously.

"Dead." There was only a slight change in her tone. "Almost four years ago. First Ma, and then Pa. Doc Doolie over at New Boston called it the summer complaint. Anyway . . ." She sat down on the milking stool and filled Gault's cup from the pot. "Anyway, within about two weeks, me and Wolf was throwed on our own. And Wolf . . ." She spread her hands and looked at them. "Wolf never was cut out to be a farmer. Claimed his hands just wouldn't fit around a hoe handle. On top of everything else, that was a dry year in Texas. Corn turned poorly and died. Most of the cotton never even sprouted." She paused and looked levelly at Gault. "Mr. Gault, do you see why I'm tellin' you all this?"

"No," Gault confessed, "I guess I don't."

"I know how hard you must feel, about your wife and all. And I guess I know that Wolf done some bad things in his time. But he was my brother, and now he's dead. And I'd give most anything I've got if I could get you to see it how it was, so that you wouldn't hate him so much and would go away and leave us alone."

Gault met those clear eyes for a moment. There didn't seem to be anything he could say. He had no wish to cause more grief for Esther Garnett, but it was highly unlikely that there was anything she could say or do that would cause him to stop hating her brother.

She sighed and gazed into space. "It's not just because of myself that I wish you'd let Wolf rest. It's mostly on your account, Mr. Gault. It's a bad thing for a man to go around with so much hate banked up inside him."

It occurred to Gault that this was a curious thing for her to say, although the thought had crossed his own mind many times. He wondered if someone had put her up to it. And if so, who? And why?

He ate half of the meat and one of the eggs and put the plate aside. She refilled his cup from the thick brew in the pot. The coffee was overroasted and bitter; the beans had been crushed Indian fashion in a limestone mortar and the resulting liquid was gritty enough to set Gault's teeth on edge. For the sake of appearances he drank part of what was in the cup, then built a smoke and lit it.

"Will you be stayin' on in Standard County, Mr. Gault? After you've mended enough to set a saddle?"

He forced a thin smile. "I don't think so. I've had enough of Sheriff Olsen's county to last me a while."

Was there a flicker of alarm in those clear eyes? "What makes you call it 'Sheriff Olsen's county'?"

He sensed that he was on thin ice. "Because he struck me as the kind of man that naturally runs things, I guess."

She nodded thoughtfully and got to her feet. "If there's anything you need, Mr. Gault . . ."

"There's something you can tell me. I'm curious about the gunhands that follow the deputy around—I'm curious about why they do it."

"Colly and Shorty?" Her tone was incredulous. "They ain't gunhands. Most of the time they work cattle, like most men hereabouts. Right now Deputy Finley's got them on as possemen. That's the deputy's right, in Standard County—hirin' possemen when he feels like he needs them."

Gault let the matter drop. He wasn't satisfied, but he had a feeling that Esther Garnett had said all she was going to say on the matter. "I'm much obliged for the breakfast, Miss Garnett."

"I'll have Shorty kill one of the old hens and cook you some chicken and dumplin's for dinner," she told him. Her eyes were so clear and youthful, and her smile so pleased, that Gault didn't have the heart to tell her that there were few things in the way of food that he detested as much as chicken and dumplings.

*

The noontime meal of chicken and dumplings arrived as promised. The dumplings were as tough as rawhide; the chicken was remarkable in that it seemed to be all bone and tendon. Gault asked, "Are the deputy and his two possemen still here?"

"Down in the bottom, thinnin' out the cotton."

"Do you work this farm all by yourself?"

She smiled wistfully. "With the help of good men like Shorty and Colly and Deputy Finley."

"Did you know Shorty and Colly when they rode with your brother?"

The smile remained at the corners of her mouth, but those blue eyes were still and thoughtful. "That's just a story folks tell. Shorty and Colly never rode with Wolf. I never saw them before . . ." She turned her head and blinked rapidly.

"Before they rode in from their trail-driving job to identify Wolf's body?" Gault was not an unfeeling man, but for this one moment he was deliberately brutal. He felt, without knowing just why, that it was important to know how Miss Garnett would react to this kind of bluntness.

She only glanced at him fleetingly and nodded. If she was offended in any way, she did not show it.

The afternoon Gault took a short turn at walking back and forth across the shed. Esther had bound his rib cage firmly, and walking was not as difficult as he had expected. He might even be able to ride for a short distance, but he was in no hurry to try it just yet.

Around midafternoon he saw Dub Finley come up from the cornfield and wash up at the Garnett well. Colly Fay brought up two horses and began saddling them. In a little while the deputy appeared in the doorway of the shed and stood there, arms folded across his chest. "Miss Esther gives you another day or so," he said, "then you'll be in shape to ride. Are you goin' to keep crowdin' your luck, Gault, or are you goin' to let Standard County alone?"

Gault gazed at the deputy and tried to size him up. He saw a brash young man who could be deadly when pushed. No doubt he was smitten with Esther Garnett's beauty and was probably in love with her. But that alone did not set him apart from other men—Gault suspected that most of the men in Standard County were in love with Esther Garnett, or thought they were. "How long have you been deputyin' for Sheriff Olsen?" Gault asked.

The question caused Finley to frown. "What makes you ask?"

"I was wonderin' if he knew he had a murderer for a deputy. Or if he knew and just didn't care."

Gault watched with interest as the deputy's face paled. His strong shoulders tensed, and for a moment Gault thought he was going for his .45. Then Shorty Pike came up behind him and said, "I'll be ready in a little while. I want to give the horses a feed before we do." With an uncurious glance at Gault, the little gunhand turned and strode back across the farmyard.

"You goin' back to New Boston?" Gault asked. "Ain't you afraid to leave me here by myself?"

The deputy looked at him and flexed his shoulders and made himself relax. "You won't be all by yourself. We're leavin' Colly back to see that you get a good start toward the Territory." He allowed himself a small smile. "Colly may not look like a man that would hold a grudge. But he'll be a long time forgettin' the way you knocked that rifle out of his hand and made him look foolish. My advice is handle him gentle and do like he tells you."

"What if I don't want to head back for the Territory?"

Finley shook his head in mock sorrow and turned from the doorway.

A few minutes later Colly brought up the saddled horses, and Finley and Shorty Pike rode back to the south. Esther Garnett stood in her back dooryard waving to them and smiling. It was a warm, common scene, one that Gault had seen hundreds of times before, and he wouldn't have thought anything about it if the two horsebackers hadn't been killers, and if the woman hadn't been the sister of Wolf Garnett.

Late that afternoon a young cowhand stopped by and spent an hour making cow eyes at Esther Garnett and helping Colly with the evening chores. Gault was beginning to understand how Miss Garnett could keep her farm in excellent repair without actually doing much of the work herself.

*

With the coming of the night the year-long rage caught fire in Gault's gut. He sat alone in the darkening shed, thinking of Martha. A blackness much blacker than the coming night, came down on him.

He did not know how long it took sleep to overtake him. But he awoke suddenly to the sound of scurrying outside the shed. A long, thin figure appeared in the doorway and slid into the darkness.

"Gault, you awake?"

The voice belonged to no one that Gault had ever heard before. "Who are you?"

"Name's Sewell. Wirt Sewell. I want to talk to you."

"What about?" Gault peered into the dark corner where the stranger was crouching, but he could see nothing of the man's face.

"Wolf Garnett," Sewell told him. "It might be we can do one another some good."

For several seconds Gault didn't even breathe. At last he said, "Move over in the light where I can see you."

The stranger hesitated, then moved into the soft moonlight that sifted through the shed's only opening. He had a hatchet face and a bobbing Adam's apple and a nose that hooked like the beak of a bald eagle. He might have been a cowhand, or a muleskinner, or just a common drifter. There was nothing special about him. "I never saw you before," Gault said.

"I seen you. Over at New Boston, talkin' to the sheriff. And I was in the crowd in front of Rucker's store when you lit off the Gainsville stage."

"You still don't tell me who you are."

The man called Sewell edged back into the shadows. "I'm an express agent. Detective, I guess you'd call me. As maybe you know, the express company had a five hundred dollar bounty on Wolf Garnett's head. That may not sound like a lot of money, but the express folks figger you got to watch the pennies if you want the dollars to take care of theirselves. Anyway, they sent me over to make sure that it was actually Wolf that the sheriff was plantin' before they turned over the money."

"Did he satisfy you it was Wolf?"

"Oh, there wasn't no doubt about that," Sewell said with a vague wave of his hand. "I wrote and told my boss that he could go ahead and pay the scalp money. That wasn't the thing that interested me."

Gault scowled. The lanky express agent was going too fast for him. "Just a minute. Did you follow me all the way from New Boston?"

"Well, more or less. I seen you pull out of town, and not

long after that I seen the deputy sheriff and his two side-men light on your trail. So I decided to follow them." His tone became slightly apologetic. "I was layin' back down-stream when the little one, the one called Shorty Pike, shot you. But there wasn't nothing I could do without givin' the game away."

"And you wouldn't want to do that," Gault said acidly. "How did you know I was interested in Wolf Garnett?"

"Everybody in New Boston that day was interested in Garnett, one way or another. Besides that, I was loafing around the livery barn that night and saw you heading off toward the graveyard."

Gault sighed to himself. "You seen a lot of things, seems like."

"It's my job. Like I say, I seen you headin' off toward the graveyard, carryin' a long-handled shovel, so I didn't have to work too hard to figger what you was up to. Did you open up the grave before the sheriff caught you?"

Gault stared at the dark figure in silence. Wirt Sewell shrugged. "Well, if you did open it, did you satisfy your-self it was Wolf Garnett?"

"I thought you was already satisfied on that score."

"I am, but it never hurts to have another opinion to lean on, when you work for a big outfit like an express com-pany. What was you lookin' for, if you don't mind sayin'?"

"I was hopin' to prove to myself that Wolf Garnett was still alive," Gault said truthfully. "When his time came to die, I wanted to be the one to kill him."

Sewell's head bobbed up and down on his long neck. "When I got your name from the wagon yard hostler it was easy to figger out who you was. There was a Gault woman that got herself killed in one of our coaches during the Garnett holdup. She was your wife?"

The question was straightforward to the point of blunt-ness. Collecting information was Sewell's job, and he had learned early that there wasn't time enough to apologize for unpleasant questions. "My wife," Gault said bleakly.

Sewell sucked in some air and it whistled through his teeth when he let it out. "I know how you feel. But Wolf's dead. Nothin' you can do about him now." He hunched his shoulders in a shrug. "All the same, there's somethin' queer."

"What do you mean?"

"I ain't sure where it begins. But for one thing, there's the county sheriff. Olsen's got a good name in these parts— and it's not a common thing for good men to put in for scalp money."

"He didn't kill anybody for it, as I understand it."

Wirt Sewell grunted. "Don't misunderstand me. There's nothin' *wrong* with takin' reward money. Federal deputies, and a lot of county lawmen, do it all the time. It's just that Olsen hisself never did it before. I wonder why he's startin' now."

"I think he aims to hand it over to Miss Garnett."

"Why'd he do a thing like that?"

"Have you ever seen Miss Garnett?"

Crouching in his dark corner, Gault sensed that the lanky express agent was smiling. "I seen her. And it might be you're right. Half the heads in New Boston was nigh twisted out of joint when the sheriff brought her to town to identify the body. I don't reckon Olsen would be the first one to let a pretty face make a fool out of him."

The two men thought about it for a moment. Gault said with a touch of dryness, "You've been watching over things since I left New Boston, seems like. Did you see the deputy's two visitors last night?"

The express agent made a startled sound. "What visitors?" He listened intently as Gault told about the arrival the night before of Olsen and the stranger. "When the storm came up," Sewell said, "I scooted back down the creekbank and throwed my bed under a rock shelf. How long was they here?"

"Two hours maybe. They pulled out before first light."

"I wish I knew who it was that Olsen had with him."

"A little stoop-shouldered geezer, that was all I could see. What do you make of it?"

The agent slumped like a poorly tied bedroll in the corner of the shed. "I don't know. I'd like to take a look inside that house."

"Not much chance. That's where Miss Garnett's sleepin'."

"Do you know where Colly Fay throwed his bed?"

Gault pointed to the main shed on the other side of the farmyard. Wirt Sewell uncoiled slowly and got to his feet. "Set easy for a few minutes. I want to take a look around." He slipped quickly through the doorway. Gault watched the slender figure mingle with dark shadows and disappear.

Several minutes passed but Sewell did not reappear. After a time it was almost possible to believe that the express agent had never existed. Gault lay back on the loose hay, every bone in his body aching. How long had it been since he had had any real rest or decent sleep? He couldn't remember.

He drifted toward unconsciousness, slowly, quietly, like a fallen leaf caught on a dark current. He thought fleetingly of Esther Garnett, but not with undue concern. He had little doubt that Miss Garnett could take care of herself. And anyway, Colly Fay was in the shed just on the other side of the farmhouse, in case Sewell was fool enough to cause trouble.

Sour with exhaustion, Gault allowed sleep to overtake him. And for once he did not dream of Martha. He dreamed of another storm. Of dark rolling clouds, and faraway lightning and thunder.

When he awoke it was daylight again. There had been

no storm. The morning was bright and clean-smelling and cool. And there was no sign of Wirt Sewell, nor could Gault discover any evidence to suggest that the lanky express agent had been there at all.

CHAPTER FIVE

Gault took some practice steps outside the shed, and Esther Garnett appeared at her kitchen door. "Seems to me like you're on the mend, Mr. Gault."

"Thanks to you, Miss Garnett," Gault said. Colly Fay appeared from a deep arroyo in the back of the house carrying a shovel.

Esther only gave Colly a casual glance. She said, "Pretty soon you'll be wantin' to leave us, I expect."

"I was thinkin'," Gault said, "that I've caused you about enough trouble. I'm much obliged for all you've done, but I'm able to ride now, any time. If Colly could help me get the buckskin saddled . . ."

In the back of Gault's memory lingered the shadowy figure of Wirt Sewell, and a puzzled expression showed in his face. Esther Garnett saw it immediately. "Is somethin' wrong, Mr. Gault?"

He couldn't bring himself to mention the mysterious express agent. He knew that Sewell had been there in the shed with him, and he knew that they had talked—he also knew that he could prove none of it.

"Nothin's wrong," he said, managing a small smile. "It was just a dream I had last night."

Those blue eyes looked at him steadily. "What kind of dream?"

"A storm. Thunder and lightnin', that kind of thing."

"There wasn't no storm last night," she told him soberly. "There was stars all over the sky. I was tellin' Colly."

"Like I say, it was just a dream." But what had happened to Wirt Sewell? He hadn't been a dream.

Gault returned to the shed, and within a few minutes Colly Fay was standing in the doorway. "Miss Esther says you're pullin' out."

"If you'll help me get the buckskin saddled."

"Which way will you be headin'?"

No sense starting a fight, Gault told himself. "Don't worry, Colly, I won't be headin' back to New Boston."

Colly brought up the saddled buckskin, then he helped Gault roll his bed and tie it on behind the cantle. "Deputy Finley said I'd get my Winchester back when I was well enough to ride out of here."

The posseman grinned. "Whatever the deputy says." He brought Gault his rifle. The firing pin had been replaced, but the magazine was empty. Gault knew without looking that the spare box of cartridges that he always carried would not be in the saddle pocket. He shoved the empty rifle into the boot.

Gault grasped the saddle horn and laboriously mounted the buckskin. The effort left him gasping. He leaned forward on the saddle horn, waiting for the pain to subside.

Colly was looking up at him, grinning widely. "You don't look too pert to me, Gault. A man in your shape, the best thing he can do is to stay out of trouble." Maybe Colly wasn't as simple as he appeared.

As Gault was pushing himself erect, Esther Garnett came out of the house carrying a grub sack. "It ain't much," she said apologetically. "Cold biscuits and dry salt meat. But maybe it'll last you till you get to your place in the Territory."

It seemed to Gault that no one ever missed an opportunity to suggest that he should make straight for Indian Territory and away from Texas. Wirt Sewell was the only one who hadn't offered some kind of argument in favor of his leaving Standard County as soon as possible—and Sewell hadn't been heard from since. "I'm much obliged for everything you've done, Miss Garnett," Gault said politely. "I'm sorry if I've put you out."

"You haven't put me out, Mr. Gault," she said with a placid smile.

The exchange was stilted and rang with false good humor. With a courteous little nod, Gault reined the buckskin away from the shed and started at an easy walk across the farmyard, heading north. He looked back once and Esther and the big posseman were deep in serious conversation. Gault rode on toward the river.

Shortly before sundown the indignant bellowing of a range cow caught Gault's attention. He reined to a knoll to see where the sound was coming from. The soft green valley of the Little Wichita was spread out in front of him, and in the center of that green carpet a man was kneeling beside a downed steer. A well-trained cow pony was standing patiently nearby.

Gault hesitated before moving in closer. If the stranger was a rustler, or an ambitious cowhand adding to his own stock, it would be smart to ride around him and pretend that he had seen nothing. But there was no branding fire that Gault could see. On impulse, he nudged the buckskin into the valley.

The man looked up at Gault. "Howdy." Then he went back to what he was doing. Beside him on the ground was an opened barlow knife, a syrup bucket half full of axle grease "dope," and a rag dauber. "Worms," the cowhand said without looking around. Meticulously, he cleaned a large sore on the steer's shoulder, cut away the proud flesh and coated the area with the black worm medicine. Finally he untied the animal and the steer loped across the valley, still bawling. The cowhand got to his feet and looked again at Gault. "You ain't from Colton, are you?"

Gault shook his head. "No."

"Colton's the straw boss. Manages the outfit for Mr. Cooper that lives in Kansas City. Hell of a way to run a cow outfit, if you was to ask me. From way off in Kansas." He put the lid on his bucket of "dope" and wrapped his dauber in a piece of tarpaulin.

"You ridin' line for Colton?" Gault asked.

The hand nodded. "South bank of the Red. Supposed to keep Cooper cattle from crossin' over and windin' up on Comanche cookin' fires. But I can't do it all myself." His tone turned to patient disgust. "Colton promised two days ago he was goin' to send me some help. You didn't see anybody along the way, have you?"

"No."

The cowhand scratched his unshaven jaw and cursed half-heartedly. "Most likely they forgot all about me." He gazed off to the south and something seemed to occur to him. "By the way," he said abruptly, "did you come by the Garnett place?"

Gault was surprised. "What makes you ask?"

"Most menfolks hereabouts wouldn't pass up a chance to see Miss Esther, if they was passin' anywheres near the place. You know Miss Esther, don't you?"

"We met," Gault said cautiously.

The cowhand grinned. "Pert as a spotted pup, ain't she? Be a powerful lucky man that gets her."

"In spite of her brother?"

The cowman waved off the notion that even an outlaw like Wolf in the family could tarnish the image of Esther Garnett. "Anyhow," he added, "Wolf's dead."

"So they say."

The cowhand wiped his hands on the seat of his worn California pants and said, "Name's Elbert Yorty."

"Frank Gault," Gault said, and vaguely embarrassed, they shook hands. Being plainsmen, they didn't ordinarily go in for handshaking, but sometimes a man, after a few weeks of talking to cows, got carried away.

"Got a piece of venison hangin' back at my line shack," Yorty said by way of invitation. "Unless you got somethin' better for supper."

Gault thought of Esther Garnett's hard biscuits and salt meat, and said gratefully, "I haven't."

On a distant knoll, directly behind Yorty, a familiar figure appeared on horseback and sat for a moment gazing down at them. Yorty didn't see him, and Gault didn't see any reason to mention it.

*

Yorty's line shack was a crude half-dugout affair nestled in the sprawling bottomland next to the Red. In Gault's honor, the cowhand carved a whole tenderloin out of the dressed venison and cooked it on a spit over a greenwood fire. "There's a monkey stove in the shack," Yorty explained, "but I never quite got the hang of cooking on it."

They ate with relish, hunkering around the fire as the cool spring night settled around them. A line rider lonesome for company, Yorty celebrated this occasion by opening a treasured can of tomatoes, and even produced some condensed milk for the coffee. In the time honored tradition of the frontier, they ate in silence, giving their entire attention to the meal at hand. Then they moved back a little from the fire and lit their smokes and sipped their scalding, faintly rancid coffee.

Gault cocked his head, listening for a moment with all his attention. If Colly was anywhere nearby he wasn't letting that fact be known. Gault thought with grim amusement that Colly must be getting pretty tired of cold grub and fireless nights.

"One lobo," Elbert Yorty was saying, "don't make a wolf pack. The Garnetts was a first-class family before Wolf started givin' it a bad name. Did you know his folks?"

"No. Esther Garnett told me her parents died four years ago."

"About that." Yorty nodded to himself. "I've been workin' cattle in Standard County longer'n I like to think about—and back in them days the Garnetts was as good as anybody in these parts. Even if they *did* start out as squatter farmers." This, from a cowman, was praise of the highest kind. "Even after Wolf started to go bad, nobody blamed it on the rest of the family. Course," he added after a moment's thought, "they was always thick as molasses."

"Who was?"

"The Garnetts. Everybody said that Miss Esther and Wolf was closer than most brothers and sisters. And the old folks, they never said anything against Wolf, even after he'd gone bad. But then, I guess nobody expected the Garnetts to say anything out loud against their own . . ."

Gault looked at his host thoughtfully. It almost seemed that Yorty was trying to tell him something without actually putting it in so many words. He said offhandedly, "Happened I was in New Boston the day of the funeral. Miss Esther didn't come."

"Pretty broke up, I guess," Yorty said, helping himself to more coffee.

"I guess." After several weeks of riding line by himself, it was clear that the cowhand was eager for human company. Still, it occurred to Gault that Yorty had talked a good deal without saying much of anything. Yorty had made no secret of his admiration for Esther Garnett, but he was no wet-nosed pup to dance a fandango—or hoe an acre of corn—just because a pretty woman smiled at him. Yorty was well into his fifties. An old man, considering the business he was in.

Gault sat for a moment, lost in his own dark memories.

Suddenly he asked, "Was you well acquainted with Wolf Garnett when he was livin' in these parts?"

"Well acquainted?" Yorty rubbed his bristling chin. "I wouldn't say that. I knowed him, like most folks did."

"Tell me about him." Gault was surprised at his own question. Until this moment his only thought had been to find Wolf Garnett and kill him.

Yorty methodically built and lit another smoke. "Not a whole lot to tell. Wolf was a bad apple from the very beginnin'. In trouble of some kind nearly all the time. Hot temper. Fist fights. A cuttin' scrape or two. But folks in Standard County figgered he was just young and a little wild. Course, it begin to look some different when we got the reports from Kansas, when he killed his first man."

"Did he ever come back to his homeplace after that?"

"Folks said he did, but I never seen him."

"Can you tell me somethin' about the county sheriff, Olsen? And the young deputy that works for him?"

Elbert Yorty finished his smoke in silence. He snapped the dead butt into the fire and said, "Don't get me wrong, I'm proud to get somebody to talk to. But it does seem like you ask some queer questions, Gault."

Gault realized that he had been pushing too hard; it was a bad habit of his. "I've got an interest in Wolf Garnett," he said slowly.

"What kind of interest?"

"Not quite a year ago he killed my wife."

Gault had not meant to put it so bluntly and coldly. But there it was, where even the dullest kind of intelligence could understand it. Now he would see just where Yorty stood.

The cowhand rocked back on his heels like an Indian and stared at him for several minutes. "I'm sorry about your wife. But I can't help you about Wolf; I already told you ever'thing I know."

"What about the sheriff?"

The cowhand spread his hands. "Nothin' there to tell. He's a good hand far's I know, and he's been on the job a long time. As for Dub Finley, he's just a young pup that likes pony hide vests and nickel-plated badges, but he'll grow out of it in time."

"Is he in love with Esther Garnett?"

The oldtimer blinked his surprise. "Maybe." Then he stretched his arms and yawned extravagantly. "It's been a long day. I think I'll throw my bed."

"Just one more thing. Deputy Finley's got two possemen riding with him. Colly Fay and Shorty Pike. Can you tell me about them?"

"Like I say," Yorty said with a humorless smile, "it's been a long day." He got to his feet and walked off toward the shack.

Gault sat for some moments in silence. Finally he got his own bed and threw it beside the fire, and for a long while he lay gazing up at the gunsteel sky while, in his mind, a driverless stagecoach went off a mountain road.

❋

Yorty was up before first light, but Gault already had the fire built and coffee water in the pot. The two men ate what was left of the venison tenderloin while the coffee boiled.

"Gault," the cowhand said in an idle tone, "I meant what I said last night, about your wife. I'm sorry. If I could help you I would, but . . ."

"But," Gault continued, "you've got your own reasons for keeping quiet. And besides, Wolf Garnett is dead."

"Well," Yorty conceded, "there's that, too. He *is* dead now. Is the rest of it so important?"

"To me it is."

The cowhand sighed. "It don't make any sense, but I guess I can understand it. But there's another reason I didn't say anything last night. Did you know we was being watched?"

"You saw him?" Gault asked in surprise.

"Heard him. Kind of scoochin' up the draw in back of the shack. Wouldn't no wild critter come up on a firelight that way. It had to be a man."

Gault smiled wearily. "One of the deputy's pals makin' sure I behave myself and leave Finley and Olsen to run the county the way they want to run it."

"I don't know about that," Yorty said, obviously puzzled. "But like I said, I guess I can understand the way you feel. About losin' your wife. So, if you feel like you just got to find out all about Wolf Garnett, there's two men you ought to talk to. First one is Harry Wompler, that used to be Olsen's deputy. Him and Esther Garnett was keepin' company till about a year ago. Some folks figgered they was aimin' to get hitched, but nothin' ever come of it."

"What happened?"

Yorty smiled crookedly. "Folks claim that Miss Esther measures her men friends against her brother and can't find one that comes up to the mark." He started to say something else, then changed his mind and gazed into the distance.

"This Wompler that used to be Olsen's deputy. How did he come to lose his job?"

Yorty's eyes became remote. "I'd rather leave that up to Wompler hisself."

"Two men, you said. Who's the other one?"

"Stock detective for the Standard County Cattlemen's Association. Name of Del Torgason."

"What makes you think Torgason would know anything about Wolf Garnett."

"It's a stock detective's business to know things. Most likely you'll find him in the Association office in New Boston."

"You still don't want to tell me how Wompler lost his badge?"

The old cowhand rubbed his jaw and considered. "Well, there was a story about Wompler gettin' hisself mixed up with a gang of rustlers. I never got all the particulars. And I guess nobody else did."

"Was Wompler arrested?"

Yorty looked as if this question had occurred to him before. "No, the sheriff just hauled him off the job and fired him."

"Is he still in New Boston?"

"Last I heard." Yorty built himself another smoke and began kicking out the fire. "You're welcome to stay around the shack, Gault, but I've got to get back on the job." He lit his smoke and asked with studied unconcern, "You aimin' to go back to New Boston and talk to Torgason and Wompler?"

"Not now. Some of the sheriff's pals are expectin' me to head back to the Territory. I wouldn't want to disappoint them."

✲

The Red was swollen with spring rains. Gault rode west, along the south bank of the river, looking for a crossing. In places the reddish water sprawled over a quarter of a mile of sandy bottomland. In the main channel, where the water was deepest, fallen cottonwoods bumped from sandbar to sandbar as they made their tortuous way downstream.

He selected a place where he knew a solid bottom of limestone existed. It was not his personal discovery, it had been discovered by the Comanches and Kiowas and Southern Cheyennes many years ago, when they were still raiding through Texas into the heart of Chihuahua.

Gault drew his Winchester from the saddle boot and put the nervous buckskin into the river. Ripples of fear passed along the animal's withers as the cold water washed his belly. The water crept higher along the stirrup leathers, but the bottom remained firm as far as mid channel. Gault took a deep breath and slid out of the saddle. The buckskin plunged into the deep water and thrashed frantically.

Gault clung to the saddle horn and held his Winchester in the air. The Winchester with the new firing pin and no ammunition. His boots filled with icy water. It lapped at his chest and soaked the elaborate bandages that Esther Garnett had applied with so much care. Then the buckskin found solid bottom again, and Gault climbed back into the saddle.

They had reached the north bank. He was now in Indian Territory—possibly in the Chickasaw Nation, but most likely in the southeast corner of the Comanche-Kiowa grasslands known to cowmen as the Big Pasture.

Gault put the buckskin up the sandy slope and stopped for a few minutes to empty his boots and squeeze some water from his windbreaker. His bedroll had been soaked in the crossing, and so had his warbag, but there was no help for that now. Sitting on a rock, he pulled on his boots and studied the south bank.

There was no sign of Colly.

Gault mounted and rode on to the north, over a string of sandhills. When he was on the far side of the hills he dismounted again and crawled up to the brush-strewn ridge and studied the south bank some more.

Apparently Colly had decided that Gault was going to be reasonable, return to his own business and put Standard County out of his thoughts.

Gault spent the rest of the morning on the north bank of the Red, watching for the big posseman while slowly drying out in the gentle sun. At last he decided that enough time had passed and that Colly had surely started back to the Garnett farm. He put the buckskin into the river again.

The buckskin hated that swift cold water even more than

Gault did. The animal's eyes rolled in fear as it scrambled for solid bottom. His small ears lay back on his head. Gault leaned forward in the saddle and stroked the quivering withers. That was when Colly Fay stepped out of a cedar thicket and said angrily, "Shorty said you'd try to slick me! And you did!"

Gault, with a sudden ache in his gut, stared at the big posseman and continued in his efforts to gentle the buckskin. Colly had his rifle aimed at Gault's chest. It was always a bad sign when a man took up his rifle instead of his revolver—the killer who meant business did not waste his time with hand guns.

Colly walked steadily toward Gault on the nervous buckskin. Gault took a deep breath and prepared to speak to the posseman in a reasonable tone. But he knew instinctively that Colly could not be reached with reason. Dull-witted men could endure almost any humiliation except the thought that they had been tricked—and this was the thought that Colly had locked into his own dull mind.

Yet, Gault heard himself saying quietly, "Colly, listen to me . . ."

But Colly wasn't listening to anyone. Gault was already as good as dead, as far as the posseman was concerned. He smiled his loose smile and came a few steps closer. Gault sat like stone. The temptation to grab for his Winchester was almost irresistible—but the rifle was useless and Colly knew it.

Then, because there seemed nothing else to do, Gault kicked his spurs into the buckskin's ribs.

The nervous animal lunged forward as if released by a spring. The slow-witted Colly stared blankly. Gault caught a glimpse of the posseman's face as the buckskin reared and crashed down on him. He was still smiling that slack smile; in his slow-moving mind he was seeing Frank Gault laid out for burying. It was probably the last thought he had, in that instant before he died.

After it was over Gault imagined that he had heard the sound of iron-shod hoofs slashing down on Colly's skull, but reason told him it was highly unlikely. It had happened too fast. The trembling buckskin had surged forward like a bullet, all but unseating Gault in the process.

There Colly had fallen beneath the buckskin's hoofs, his shabby hat crushed down over his bloody face. Gault did not have to look a second time to know that he was dead. He spurred the animal away from the scene. For several seconds he sat bent over the saddle horn, his insides strangely cold, his stomach pushing into his throat.

For almost a year Gault's thoughts had been concerned exclusively with the subject of death. In his dreams, waking and sleeping, he had killed Wolf Garnett a thousand times. But it had never been like this, with the crunch of bone and rush of blood. In his mind it had always been swift and clean and right.

He kneed the buckskin into a gully where the corpse could not be seen nor the blood smelled, and then he slowly dismounted and tied up in a flowering redbud. He knew that he would have to go back and do something about the body. But at the moment he didn't want to think about it.

So he stayed with the buckskin, gentling the animal until it stood calmly. Only then did he make himself return to that sandy flat where the body lay. "I didn't aim to kill you, Colly," he heard himself saying aloud. "Even though," the voice continued, "you sure as hell was aimin' to kill me."

He still wasn't sure what ought to be done about the body. Bury it? He had nothing to dig with. Take it with him to New Boston? He smiled grimly at the thought of bringing in one of Olsen's possemen, like a dog with a bone, and laying it at the big lawman's feet.

He postponed the decision by tramping downstream to where Colly had staked his own animal. He pulled the stake pin and gentled the posseman's black gelding. Almost as an afterthought, and without much hope, he began searching the saddle pockets for ammunition to fit his Winchester.

He gave a little grunt of surprise as he pulled out a full box of .30 caliber shells. Maybe his luck was changing. He dug deeper in the saddle pocket and lifted out a carefully wrapped parcel, a package several times the size of the shell box, wrapped with considerable care in a flannel shirt and an oilskin covering. But in spite of the care that had gone into the wrapping, one end had come open. As Gault took the parcel in his hands two gold double-eagles spilled out and fell to the ground. Colly Fay was still full of surprises.

Gault hunkered down beside the gelding and carefully opened the package. For a long while he remained in that position, staring down at the contents. A yellow gold watch, and a heavy chain of the same metal. A silver penknife. Several loose coins, including four more double-eagles. A roll of greenbacks wrapped in its own protective oilskin cover. Gault unwrapped it and counted them—they came to three hundred and ninety dollars.

There was also a small buckskin pouch which Gault opened and emptied onto the oilskin. One by one, he ticked off the small items in his mind. A pair of earrings set with small stones that might have been diamonds. A string of milky white beads that could have been pearls. And at the bottom of the buckskin pouch there was a plain rose gold wedding band. It was the ring that Gault had given to Martha when they were married.

Gault could not remember how long he crouched there, holding that small ring in his hand, trying to feel something of his lost wife in the rose-colored metal. But Martha was a year dead almost. There was nothing of her in the ring.

Still he crouched there, staring out at the sprawling sandy banks of the Red. He remained so still that a squirrel darted out of a liveoak tree and scurried in front of him without seeing him. It was almost as if he had been captured there in a block of invisible ice, seeing nothing, hearing nothing, aware of nothing but that small gold ring.

The black gelding tugged at its stakerope. Gault turned and looked at the animal as if he were seeing it for the first time. Slowly, he dropped the ring into his shirt pocket. Then he rewrapped the small parcel with the same great care that Colly had taken in wrapping it for the first time.

Finally he led the black to the gully where the buckskin was waiting. Then he walked back to where the dead man lay sprawled in the sand.

"Time to get up, Colly. We're going to New Boston."

CHAPTER SIX

It was early afternoon and the town was quiet when Gault entered it. Much quieter than it had been on the day of the funeral. Farmers were back working their crops. Stockmen were finishing up their spring branding. A slack day in a slack season. A town dozing beneath a gentle North Texas sun.

The hostler at the wagon yard was the first to see them. The little bandy-legged man came pushing a wheelbarrow of manure around the corner of the livery barn when he first saw Gault slouched wearily on the buckskin. Colly's black gelding plodded behind on a lead rope, with the dead posseman across the saddle.

The hostler, whose name was Abe Tricer, dropped the wheelbarrow and started running toward the center of town. Gault watched him without expression.

A curious storekeeper stepped out to the sidewalk to see what the running was about. He took one look at Gault and the burdened black and called to someone in the store. By the time Gault reached the general store where the sheriff had his office, there were several little clusters of men gathered on the sidewalk. They did not venture away from the storefronts but stood quietly, watching.

The sheriff and the little hostler appeared in the doorway

of Olsen's office as Gault tied up in front of the store. The big lawman stepped out on the second-floor gallery and looked down at them with thunder in his face. He came down the stairway two steps at a time.

"What's goin' on here?" he snarled.

"Your posseman's dead. I brought him home," Gault said with a flatness of tone that caused the sheriff to blink. Then Olsen strode to the black, lifted the dead man's head and studied the dead face. "He's not my posseman."

"Your deputy's, then. It comes to the same thing."

The little hostler was fairly dancing with excitement. "I was the first one seen him, Sheriff. Come ridin' into town, just like he owned it. I recognized Colly's black geldin' right off. Recognized Colly too. Dead as a fencepost. I'd figgered you'd want to know about it right off."

"See if you can find Doc Doolie," Olsen said.

"What you want with the doc? Colly's done for. Don't take a doc to see that."

"Get him." This time there was no nonsense in Olsen's voice. "The rest of you . . ." He raked the gathering of loafers and storekeepers and a scattering of cowhands. "Get back to whatever you was doin'."

The hostler made for the upper end of the street in a rolling, lurching lope of the oldtime horseman. The rest of the crowd began backing up, reluctantly. They were curious to see what was going to develop, but none of them was anxious to tangle with Grady Olsen.

"You," the sheriff said harshly to Gault. "Give me a hand here."

Together they slipped the dead posseman off the saddle and laid him out beside Rucker's store. "Have you got a tarp or somethin' to cover him with?" the sheriff asked.

"No."

Glaring, Olsen returned to the gelding, unsaddled the animal and covered the dead man with the saddle blanket.

Then he pointed toward the stairway. "Up to my office. I'll talk to you there."

Inside the combination office-living quarters the sheriff slumped behind the oilcloth-covered table and motioned Gault to a chair. As Gault sat down somewhat cautiously, Olsen noticed for the first time that his face was pale and drawn beneath the stubble of trail beard. "You ailin' with somethin', Gault?"

"I'm fine," Gault said gratingly, "except for a busted rib, that comes from bein' shot by another one of your possemen. But I guess you got the whole story about that—when you rode out to the Garnett farm the night of the storm."

Gault watched him closely, wondering what his reaction would be. But Olsen only sat looking at him, his expression unchanging.

The lawman picked up a stub of a pencil and began turning it over and over in his blunt fingers. "My deputy told me about the shootin'," he said coldly. "Accident. Too bad it happened, but that's the way it goes when you mess with things that's none of your business. Anyway . . ." He made a motion with one hand, waving the subject away. "Anyway, that ain't the thing we're concerned with right now. You just brought me a dead man." His eyes narrowed. "Did you kill him?"

Gault breathed as deeply as he could against the tight bandaging. "Yes."

The sheriff blinked owlishly. "Why?"

The question was not as simple as it might first appear, and Gault was aware of it. "For one thing, he was about to kill me."

"Why would Colly Fay want to kill you?"

"He thought I wanted to trick him—and Colly couldn't stand the notion of somebody trying to make him look foolish. Anyway, he had orders to see that I returned to the

Territory. When I came back across the river, that's when he tried to kill me."

The big sheriff shot him a bleak look. "I don't guess there was any witnesses that could testify it was an accident?"

"No. But there was this." Gault dug the flannel-wrapped parcel from the pocket of his windbreaker. He put it on the table. "When it was over, I went lookin' for Colly's horse. This is what I found in the saddle pocket."

Olsen looked at the package but did not touch it. Gault went on. "I'm not such a fool that I didn't realize it would be a dangerous proposition, me comin' back to New Boston with a dead posseman across his saddle. Common sense told me to roll him in a gully and pile rocks on top of him and put him out of my mind. That package he was carryin' made the difference. It's the reason I brought him back."

Olsen touched the parcel as he might have touched the clothing of a cholera patient. With thumb and forefinger he unfolded the flannel envelope. For some time he sat gazing at the gold watch and the string of milky pearls. His attention returned to the watch and he sat gazing bleakly at the curious inscription on the face cover.

At last the sheriff opened the buckskin pouch and emptied the contents on the table. He nudged the earrings with their glittering little diamonds over toward the pearls. The gold coins he counted and stacked neatly beside the greenbacks. When he had thoroughly memorized every detail of every article, he picked up the watch and studied it some more. "Is this all?"

"Except for this." Gault showed him the small band of gold. "I didn't think you'd mind if I kept it. It belonged to my wife."

The sheriff's mouth came open, but for the moment he did not speak. He slowly digested the meaning of the ring as a silent wall of hostility built up between them.

Doc Doolie appeared in the doorway, and the sheriff asked, "Did you look at Colly?"

"I looked at him. Been dead about a day, best I could tell. Skull busted in—looks like a horse kicked him." The little doc came into the room, took a kitchen chair and sat at the end of the sheriff's table. Gault stared at him so steadily and so hard that Doolie began to frown.

For a moment Gault had been startled to see the doc standing there. A small, slightly stooped figure. There was a shadow of such a figure still lodged in a back chamber of his mind. For the best part of three days he had been wondering about the man who had come to the Garnett farm with the sheriff on the night of the storm. That man had been Dr. Marvin Doolie.

The doc was beginning to be irritated by Gault's unblinking staring. "If you got somethin' in your craw, mister," he snapped, "spit it out."

"I was wonderin'," Gault said bluntly, "what you and the sheriff was doin' at the Garnett place in the middle of the night." Gault had to count back in his mind. How long had it been? "Three nights ago."

Doolie came stiffly erect and glanced at Olsen. But the sheriff folded his hands placidly and said, "Mr. Gault has got a suspicious mind, Doc. And I guess we can't blame him too much. For nearly a year he's been runnin' in hard luck, and then, to set things off, he went and got hisself shot by Shorty Pike. Accident, of course."

Doolie nodded. "Shorty told us about that. Misunderstandin' about some Garnett cows, wasn't it? Hard luck— but that's the kind of thing that happens when you stray on the other fellow's range."

"Maybe," Gault said dryly. "Whatever the reason, I did get myself shot. Now I'm wonderin' why you didn't bother to come and have a look at me, long as you was on the place anyway. You *are* a doc, ain't you?"

Doolie flushed pink and glanced at the sheriff for guidance. "And a first-class doc at that," Olsen said blandly. "If you'd needed lookin' at, he would of looked at you. But

Miss Esther said you was doin' fine and there wasn't no use botherin' you."

Gault smiled at them. "I see. But you still haven't said what you were doin' on the prairie in the middle of the night, in a thunderstorm."

Doolie smiled as though the effort pained him. "Maybe that's because it's none of your business, Mr. Gault. However . . ." He glanced at the sheriff, and Olsen nodded ever so slightly. "However, I don't mind tellin' you. A hand over at Circle-R headquarters got hisself busted up when a horse fell on him, and I was tendin' him. On the way back to town there was the thunderstorm, so we stopped by the Garnett place to dry out."

Gault looked at them. The little doc had, more or less, explained his own movements. Sheriff Grady Olsen, apparently, did not feel obligated to explain his movements to anyone. In a tone that was bland to the point of indifference, the lawman asked, "Doc, what do you make out of this?"

Doolie leaned forward and stared at the articles on the table. He picked up the gold watch and inspected it minutely. After a long silence he turned his attention to the pearls. "One of the passengers on the Fort Belknap stage that was held up—didn't she report losin' a string of beads like this?"

The sheriff's head dropped in a heavy nod. "I figgered the same thing when I seen it. I'll get a letter off to that express agent. What was his name?"

"Sewell," Gault said without thinking. "Wirt Sewell."

Something happened behind the sheriff's eyes. "I didn't know you and Sewell was acquainted."

Now it was Gault's turn to act mysterious, and he took a grim pleasure in watching the lines of concern form around Olsen's eyes. "We met," he said shortly. He leaned forward and suddenly his voice came out harsh and angry. "You've worn a badge a long time, Sheriff. Long enough to know what this means." He pointed to the articles on the table. "These things tie Colly Fay to a stage robbery. And Shorty Pike ties to Colly, and both of them tie to your deputy who put them on his payroll. In one way or another, that connects the sheriff's office with Wolf Garnett . . . and the death of my wife."

Olsen made a rumbling sound in his throat. He kicked back his chair and stood up. "I know how you feel about your wife, but that don't give you any right to lay the blame on this office. I'm warnin' you, don't dip your horns in my business."

Gault pushed his own chair back and stood up. "This makes it my business," he said, showing the small gold ring. When he got to the doorway he turned for a moment and asked, "How about that .45 of mine?"

"I'll ask my deputy where he put it. When I see him."

*

Gault entered the Day and Night Bar with his Winchester cradled in the crook of his right arm. He paid for a schooner of sour beer and said, "I want to talk to Harry Wompler."

The barkeep, a fat, sleepy-eyed ex-muleskinner, looked him over carefully. Gault had learned early that Wompler was not an easy man to locate. For more than an hour he had been passed from saloon to saloon, and now he was at the end of the line, in the dirt-floored Day and Night.

"Take a beer for yourself," Gault said blandly. "And draw one for Harry." He put some silver on the bar.

"You a pal of Harry's?"

"Not a pal, exactly. But we may have the same enemies."

The barkeep grinned and drew himself a beer. It was clear that any enemy of Olsen's was a friend of the barkeep's. "There's Harry Wompler, over in the corner, but don't be surprised if he won't talk to you. Harry ain't been none too sociable since he lost his deputy's badge. Put great store in that nickel-plated star, Harry did, before Grady Olsen took it away from him."

The former deputy sheriff of Standard County lay face-down across the table, his head on his arms, snoring lustily. Gault put a beer on the table and pulled up a chair. "I want to talk to you, Wompler."

Harry snorted and grunted and went on with his snoring.

"About Grady Olsen." Gault shook him gently. Wompler's head dangled lifelessly on his scrawny neck. He snored on.

"And Wolf Garnett."

Harry didn't budge. Gault shoved the full schooner toward him and said, "I brought you a beer."

A muscle alongside the former deputy's neck began to twitch. He lifted his head and stared blearily at Gault. He pulled the beer to him, with all the tenderness of a new mother holding her first child, and he fumbled it to his mouth and drank steadily until the heavy glass mug was empty.

"Who are you?"

"Frank Gault. An old line rider called Yorty told me to look you up when I got to New Boston. I'm tryin' to find out about Wolf Garnett."

"Find out what?"

Gault couldn't bring himself to talk about Martha in a place like the Day and Night. "It's personal." Then, because Wompler seemed to be drifting back to sleep, he asked, "Can I buy you another beer?"

Harry nodded heavily, as if he were carrying the weight of the world on the back of his neck. "Make it whiskey."

The barkeep knew his customers well. He had already set two glasses and a full bottle on the table. The former deputy forced himself erect, sloshed some whiskey into a glass and downed it. "Nothin' to tell," he said haltingly, like a crippled man learning to walk. "About Wolf Garnett. He's dead."

"About the sheriff then?"

Wompler stared at him for a full minute without making a sound. He was a youngish man, still in his twenties. Once he might have been considered handsome, but a steady diet of the Day and Night's raw corn whiskey had taken care of that. His lower lip protruded curiously, giving him a pouting look. His face bristled with a week's growth of beard, but it was round and strangely youthful. He looked, Gault thought, to himself, like a sixty-year-old baby with pouchy eyes. "Why," he asked, "do you want to know about the sheriff?"

"I think he's mixed up somehow with the Wolf Garnett bunch. What's left of the bunch, anyway."

Wompler stared at him, blinking his watery eyes. Suddenly he began laughing. The sound was eerily hollow coming out of that bearded baby face.

Gault's own voice turned cold. "I didn't know I'd said somethin' funny."

"You did, though. I din't think there was a man in Standard County—or Texas, for that matter—that didn't know about Grady Olsen and the Garnetts." He poured himself another drink and Gault noticed that his hands were steadier now.

"Tell me about them."

"Simplest thing in the world. For four years Olsen's been makin' moon eyes at Esther Garnett. Him old enough to be her pa. And then some."

Gault stared at the derelict in amazement. Since the night of the thunderstorm he had often tried to explain the sheriff's odd behavior—but this possibility had not occurred to him. "Olsen's in love with Miss Garnett?"

"Like a moon-eyed calf." Harry helped himself to another drink. "It's the reason he fired me."

The story was taking some unexpected turns. Grinning loosely, Wompler wiped his mouth with the back of his hand and said, "Me and Esther—I guess ever'body in the county knowed she took a shine to me. That's why he had to get me out of the way. Took away my badge." The old baby face turned ugly. "I guess that ain't the way you heard it, though."

"I heard that Olsen let you go for bein' too thick with a gang of rustlers."

Wompler's eyes were losing their focus. "Believe anything you please. It's all the same to me."

Gault sat for a moment digesting what he had heard. "Do you know a stock detective named Del Torgason?"

"Torgason?" Wompler's tongue was beginning to thicken. "Torgason and me are the only ones in Standard County that'll talk back to Olsen."

"Why would Torgason want to make an enemy of the sheriff?"

"It ain't that he wants to. He just don't give a damn. The big men in this part of Texas are the cowmen, and they're the ones that pay his salary. Not even Olsen would go out of his way to rile a cowman."

"I was beginning to get the feelin' that everybody in the county kowtowed to Olsen. The cowmen don't?"

"Cowmen," the former lawman smiled slackly, "don't kowtow to anybody."

"Where can I find Torgason?"

Wompler sensed that the period of free liquor was about to end. Quickly, he sloshed himself another drink. "In the Association office, if he's in town. At the far end of the street, over the bath house."

The bath house occupied a space in the broad back alley behind the New Boston Gentlemen's Barber Shop. The county office of the cattlemen's association was a boxlike structure atop the bath house, sitting alongside a metal hot water tank. It was reached by an outside stairway, as were most second story establishments in New Boston.

Gault climbed the stairs and stepped through the open doorway. There was a rolltop desk, a battered oak chair. On the plank wall there was a large calendar for the year

1882, an advertisement for Dr. J. J. Simpson's Electric Bitters. Beside the calendar, dangling from a length of bit chain, was a North Texas Stock Raisers' Brand Book. There was no sign of stock detective Del Torgason.

A handyman from the bath house came up the stairway with an armload of cowchips and dumped them into the firebox beneath the hot water tank. Gault stepped out to the landing and asked, "Can you tell me where to find Torgason?"

The handyman looked him over. "Who's askin'?"

"My name's Frank Gault."

That was all the handyman needed to know. "Nope," he said shortly, and stumped back down the stairs. It was clear that the sheriff had not been pleased by Gault's return to New Boston, and it hadn't taken long for the word to get around. Gault picked up the buckskin and moved on to the wagon yard.

The hostler, Abe Tricer, was waiting for him with a vindictive grin. "Sorry, Gault, I just rented out the last of my camp shacks."

The shacks stood against the livery barn with their doors wide open and obviously vacant. "How about I throw my bed in the loft."

"Town passed an ordinance against that."

"Ordinance?"

"Drifters sleepin' in the loft like to burn the place down."

Gault knew it would be useless to argue the matter. "Do you think you could feed and water the buckskin?"

The hostler shrugged. "Price of oats has gone up since the last time you was through here."

"Somehow," Gault told him, "I figgered it would." He stripped the buckskin and put the animal in a stall. Then he returned to the Day and Night.

Wompler was at the same table, staring into space. Only after Gault set a full bottle in front of him did he begin to look alive. "Torgason ain't in his office," Gault said. "I tried askin' some New Boston citizens about him, but it didn't get me anywhere."

Wompler downed a drink and chuckled. "They know the sheriff wouldn't like it. And what Sheriff Olsen don't like we don't get much of, here in Standard County."

"You know where I might find Torgason?"

The former deputy closed his eyes, and for a moment Gault was afraid he'd fallen asleep. At last he said, "This mornin' I was down at the livery corral. Torgason came by to get his horse. There was somethin' said about the Circle-R."

The name had a familiar ring. The oldtime cowhand, Elbert Yorty, rode line for the Circle-R. Also it had been an injured Circle-R hand that Doc Doolie had been tending the night of the thunderstorm—according to Doc Doolie. "Is there anything queer about the Circle-R? Or about Torgason heading that way today?"

Wompler looked at him blearily. "Nothin' I can think of."

"You ever have any trouble with the outfit, when you was deputy?"

The ex-lawman shook his head. "Nope. What you lookin' for?"

It was a reasonable question, but Gault didn't have a reasonable answer. What was he looking for? Gault only knew that the fire in his gut wouldn't let him rest until something was done. "What I'm lookin' for is not something I can put a finger on. It's a feelin'."

"About the sheriff?"

Gault nodded. "That's part of it."

"Is it true what they're sayin'? That Wolf Garnett killed your wife?"

The former deputy, Gault decided, was more alert than he appeared to be. "It's true." He waited a full minute for Wompler to go on, but the ex-lawman only shrugged and let the matter drop. Gault said, "What's the best way for me to get to the Circle-R? I want to talk to Torgason."

"He's close-mouthed. You won't get much out of him, even if he knowed somethin' to tell." Wompler brightened slightly as a thought occurred to him. "Have you got the money to pay for a rent animal over at the livery corral?"

"I guess so. Why?"

"If there's a chance of puttin' somethin' over on Olsen, I'd like to deal myself in. You pay for the rent animal and I'll ride with you to the Circle-R." Gault hesitated, and Wompler added flatly, "I ain't as useless as I might look. I can use a gun, if I have to."

Gault was vaguely disturbed by the way he said it. "Do you expect to have to?"

"Don't expect nothin' but tricks and slick dealin' when doin' business with Grady Olsen. Will you pay for the horse?"

Wompler was not the kind of man that Gault would have chosen to ride with. But he found himself nodding, reluctantly.

Wompler sighed, smiled crookedly, and with considerable effort pushed himself to his feet. "One more thing," he said, tucking the bottle of liquor under his arm. "You might pay the barkeep for this."

Against his better judgment, Gault paid for the whiskey. They left the Day and Night and walked the short distance to the wagon yard. The exertion left Wompler winded, but his watery eyes had cleared a bit and his speech was not so slurred. "Of course," the former deputy said, "I don't aim to drink this down all at once." He fondly caressed the bottle. "It's just that I've been promisin' myself for a long time that I'd kill Grady Olsen if I ever got the chance. And I might just do it if I was to catch myself completely sober."

CHAPTER SEVEN

Headquarters for the Circle-R was a scattering of sheds and branding pens and corrals, an hour's ride from New Boston. There was no owner's "big house," as the owner rarely visited the place. The manager lived with the hands in a split-pole bunkhouse.

Such a spread was not impressive, but there were a number of them on the plains below the Cap Rock. When well managed they were efficient and productive and made money for the owner who might live as far away as England or Scotland and never get within five thousand miles of his holdings. An aging wrangler appeared from behind a brush-covered shed and met them as they headed for the main buildings. The old man glared at Gault with distrust, but his reaction to Wompler was undisguised anger.

Wompler smiled his meaningless smile and said, "Seth here is Colton's headquarters wrangler and cook. This is Frank Gault, Seth. We're lookin' for Del Torgason."

The old man glared at Wompler and suddenly spat at the ground in disgust. "I don't make it a habit to socialize with cow thieves!"

"Seth," Wompler went on with a disinterested air, "firmly believes that up to a year ago I headed a rustlin' operation here in Standard County. That's what most folks believe, I guess." He spread his hands and smiled benignly down at the old man. "Well, it was never proved, and anyhow it's water over the dam. Just tell us where to find Torgason."

The wrangler jutted his jaw defiantly. "Torgason went out with the boss, Mr. Colton. I don't know where."

Wompler's tone turned menacing. "Mr. Gault here is a beef buyer for the Kiowa-Comanche agency. Mr. Colton won't like it, missin' a big beef sale, just because he's got a stubborn old wrangler on the place."

The old man paled. He knew very well that a missed sale could mean his job. And for men his age even wrangler jobs were next to impossible to come by. "Last I seen of Mr. Colton," he said shakily, "him and two hands and Torgason was headed toward north camp, brandin' strays they missed in the roundup."

"We're much obliged for all your help, Seth," Wompler said with heavy sarcasm. He reined his rented black gelding around the old man and headed north. Gault, after an instant's hesitation, followed on the buckskin.

"Was it necessary," Gault asked angrily, "to scare the old man like that?"

"Yes," Wompler said. "As you'll learn, Gault, it's the only way to get anywheres in Standard County. Fear. It's a little lesson I learned when I was deputyin' for Grady Olsen."

*

By sundown Gault was tired of the saddle and sick of the company of Harry Wompler. They arrived at the banks of the Little Wichita as the sun was touching the dark green horizon. "We can make camp here," the ex-deputy said. "Or we can make it on to the Circle-R camp in maybe another hour."

Gault's side was aching. "We'll camp here. I've had enough of the saddle for one day." They staked the horses downstream, boiled coffee and ate what was left in Gault's grub sack.

Wompler held one heavy biscuit to the fading light and said, "Don't have to ask where you got these. Esther never was no prize as a cook. Even I would admit that much."

"Did you know Miss Garnett long?"

The ex-deputy smiled his slack smile. "Long enough."

They finished the meal in silence, then Wompler dug the bottle out of his saddlebag and downed a carefully measured ration of whiskey. He put the bottle away without offering it to Gault. A faded army blanket and a yellow slicker known as a "fish" had come with Wompler's rented horse and saddle. He dumped it beneath the budding branches of a cottonwood, then walked up the grade from the river and stood for a while, building and smoking his highly combustible cigarettes, gazing upstream toward the Garnett place.

Gault decided the former lawman was not an easy man to know. In the Day and Night he had been a common drunk. At the Circle-R headquarters he had been ill-tempered and brutal to the old wrangler. Since that time he had shown flashes of sensitivity and the rudiments of education, neither of which were very common in a place like Standard County.

Gault sat beside the dying fire, smoking, trying to keep his mind away from the past. Wondering what he was going to say to the stock detective, Torgason, when he found him. How could Torgason help him? How could anybody help him?

When Wompler came back down the slope and stood beside the fire, Gault said, "Tell me about Torgason."

"Torgason . . ." Wompler considered his subject. "He's an old hand, good at his job, no nonsense. I don't like him, but he knows his business. And he ain't afraid of Olsen." With a curt nod, Wompler got to his feet and went to his bedroll. Tugging off his boots, he said, "You might not think it, Gault, but I used to be a man of ambition. I read law with old Judge Tabor at Gainsville. I set myself the task of learnin' the law, and then politics, and then . . ." Gault could not see his face, but he knew that Wompler was smiling that loose-lipped smile of his. "There wasn't no limit to the ambition I had in those days. A year ago I lost more than a job and a woman. I lost the man that used to be Harry Wompler. And I guess I won't be satisfied until I find out where he went."

●

During the night Gault came suddenly awake. Wompler was snoring. Far to the north a spring storm was passing. Silent lightning blinked in the distance.

Lightning . . .

Frowning, Gault rubbed his hands over his face. He sat for a long while, thinking, as a damp chill worked its way into his bones. Had it been a dream that had shocked him awake? He could remember no dream—and Lord knew he had no trouble remembering the nightmares of the past. No, he was convinced that it had not been a dream.

He pulled the blanket around him and continued to sit there beside the dead fire. Had it been a noise that had wakened him? Something, or someone, coming up on their camp?

No . . . He shook his head, staring at the distant lightning. Then, very faintly, he heard the thunder, rolling over the prairie so far away that it was hardly a sound at all.

Thunder . . . For a moment the thought hung there.

"It wasn't thunder that night," he said aloud. "It was a gun."

Wompler rolled over and raised himself on one elbow. "You talkin' to me?"

"No. I was thinkin' out loud." Then, still thinking it out in speech, he said, "The next mornin' there was Shorty Pike comin' out of the arroyo with the shovel. He killed him, and down there somewhere is where he buried him."

Wompler threw off his blanket. "Shorty Pike killed somebody and buried him in an arroyo?"

"An express agent named Wirt Sewell." Gault was trying to pull together the loose ends. "I was talkin' to Sewell that night. He had his suspicions about the new deputy and his possemen, so when Deputy Finley and his sidekicks followed me out of New Boston, he followed all of us. And we all wound up at the Garnett place. Me with a bullet graze and a busted rib. But I never saw him after that talk . . ." He could still see that lanky figure hunkered in the dark corner of the shed.

"Never saw who?"

"The express man. After I went back to sleep there was another thunderstorm. But next mornin' the ground was dry, so I figgered it was a dream. But it wasn't a dream, it was a gunshot. Not thunder. And that morning Shorty Pike was comin' out of the arroyo with a long-handled shovel in his hand."

Harry Wompler gave a snort of exasperation, and Gault went back to the beginning, back to the moment when Wirt Sewell had first appeared in the doorway of the shed. He recreated the scene word for word, as well as he could remember it, and Wompler did not interrupt until he had finished. Then he said, "I think we better have a drink."

The former deputy brought the bottle to the dead fire and the two men drank silently. Wompler shook the bottle sadly; it was almost empty. "It sounds loco," he said. "Maybe that's why I believe it. Folks told me I was loco, too, when I tried to convince them I had nothin' to do with cattle rustlers."

"What did the cattlemen think about it?" This was something that Gault had wondered about for some time.

Wompler turned up the bottle, had another swallow and

corked it. "Cowman is a contrary critter. Sometimes he goes off on a short fuse. Sometimes, if you get his suspicions up, he'll dog you like a Kiowa tracker. But there's one thing you can bank on—if the cowmen was sure I was in with rustlers, I'd of been hung months ago. I figger they've turned it over to Torgason and his Association, to find out for sure."

"Can Torgason get to the bottom of it?"

"If anybody can." Wompler shrugged.

At first light they rolled their beds and started upstream.

*

They topped the grassy rise near the place where Gault had been shot by Shorty Pike. For several minutes they sat their horses, studying the placid scene before them. A young cowhand, his pony tied to a fencepost, had stopped off long enough to chop a few rows of cotton. The fields were neat and sparkling. The yard and sheds appeared well kept.

"One thing about Esther," Wompler said ruefully, "she never had no trouble keepin' the place in shape. Always a cowhand or one of the sheriff's men stoppin' by to help out." Then, as they watched, Esther Garnett stepped out of a shed and began scattering feed to a small flock of chickens. Wompler came erect in his saddle, his face stiff and cold. Then, slowly, he began to relax. "The wrong kind of woman," he said flatly, "is a good deal like the wrong kind of whiskey. Poison to the system. But," he added with a cold smile, "a man gets over it in time." He pointed toward the deep wash behind the farmhouse. "Is that where you figger the express agent is?"

"That's where I saw Shorty comin' from."

They put their horses down the slope, out of sight of the house, and walked the rest of the way to the arroyo. They stood for several minutes on the edge of the gully. The bottom was strewn with casual rubbish, along with the cleanings of the barn and chicken house, waiting for the next spring flood to wash it away. There was nothing that looked like a grave.

"You sure this is the place?" Wompler asked doubtfully.

"Maybe it's farther down toward the river." He started to climb down into the wash when the former lawman caught his arm.

"One thing I learned settin' in the Day and Night for almost a year, and that's to be suspicious. If you're goin' to scout the gully, I'll keep watch up here with the rifle."

Gault didn't like parting with his Winchester, but he handed it over and accepted Wompler's .45 in exchange. "Keep an eye on the house, in case Deputy Finley's put on more possemen." He slid into the wash.

For the best part of an hour Gault explored the arroyo. At last, beneath a stinking pile of straw from a cow stall, he found freshly dug earth. He looked up at Wompler. "I think we've found Wirt Sewell."

Wompler didn't look convinced, but he said, "Find somethin' to dig with. I'll keep an eye on the Garnett place."

With a broken plow-handle Gault began gouging at the loose earth. Soon the jagged tip of the plow-handle struck something foreign to the loosely packed clay. It was a sensation that set Gault's skin crawling; he had experienced it once before while digging in the graveyard west of New Boston.

Wompler crouched on the lip of the wash. Slowly, Gault began clearing away some of the loose clay. What he had unearthed was not the missing express agent but the brown and white flank of a spotted calf.

Wompler slid into the wash for a closer look. "Well," he said, breaking an uneasy silence, "maybe Shorty wasn't buryin' the express agent after all."

"Why would he go to the trouble of buryin' a calf? When a cow gets itself killed on the prairie, you leave it where it falls. Unless it's diseased, then you burn it."

"That's what a cowman would do. These are farmers—and sometimes there's no explainin' the things a sodbuster will do." The former deputy began kicking dirt back into the hole. "Maybe Esther took the calf as a pet, and couldn't bear to leave it for the buzzards. There's no explainin' women, either."

Gault smiled grimly. "It still doesn't tell me what happened to that express agent."

The two men finished filling the hole and climbed out of the wash. Wompler built himself a smoke and said, "You want to turn around and see if we can find Torgason and the Circle-R branding crew?"

Gault was reluctant to leave the farm, but he could think of no good reason for lingering there; he was no pink-cheeked cowhand looking for excuses to moon over Esther Garnett.

Wompler tramped into the river underbrush where he had tied the horses. In a few minutes he came back leading the animals, and Gault was quick to notice the pinched look of apprehension about the ex-deputy's eyes. "Might be," he said quietly, "we got ourselves some trouble. Somebody's watchin' us. Back there in the brush."

Gault studied the thicket from beneath the brim of his hat. "I don't see anything."

"He's there." Wompler wiped the back of his hand across his mouth. "You think it's Shorty Pike? He's already had one try at killin' you; maybe he's lookin' to finish the job."

"Maybe . . ." Gault took the buckskin's reins and quickly put the animal between himself and the thicket, a common-sense precaution that Harry Wompler had already attended to. They began walking their horses away from the arroyo. Of course, Gault thought bleakly, there's nothin' to keep him from shootin' the horses first, then us.

A voice from the direction of the brush called, "Hold up, Wompler. You too, mister, whoever you are."

Gault grasped the buckskin's bitchain and froze. He shot

a look at Wompler and was relieved to see the beginning
of that familiar slack-mouthed smile.

"We won't have to go lookin' for Torgason. He's found
us."

Gault moved the buckskin aside and watched the tall,
sunbrowned man coming out of the thicket. He carried a
Winchester saddle rifle in one hand, cocked and ready to
fire, as if it had been a Buntline pistol. He looked to be in
his middle thirties, lean, tough, all business. He had a
wooden, Indianlike face, and Gault got the feeling that it
would shatter like overheated flint if he ever tried smiling.

"Good luck you found us," Wompler said easily. "We was
about to go lookin' for you."

"Why?" Torgason eased the Winchester's hammer to half
cock and cradled the weapon in his arm.

"This here's Frank Gault. He's got kind of a personal
interest in the Garnetts. But maybe you better let him tell
you about it."

Standing there beside the arroyo, Gault told the Association man everything he knew or suspected. About Martha, and Sewell, and Colly Fay. About getting himself shot
by Shorty Pike, on Deputy Finley's orders. About the
dreamed thunderstorm that appeared to be neither dream
nor storm. About Shorty with the shovel, and the buried
calf.

Torgason heard him out without the slightest change in
expression. "What makes you think I can help you?"

"An oldtime line rider, name of Yorty, thought you might
be the one to talk to."

Torgason studied him disinterestedly. Never a word of
sympathy when he heard about Martha. A man of business
was Del Torgason, and that business was seeing that the
cattlemen of Standard County were kept happy and the
county reasonably free of rustlers. "Elbert Yorty," he said
bluntly, "is an old fool. I've got no quarrel with the sheriff.

My advice, Gault, is go back to where you came from and leave Standard County to look after itself."

Gault smiled thinly. "I get a lot of that kind of advice."

The stock detective shrugged his wide shoulders, a picture of total indifference. "A thunderstorm that's not a thunderstorm. A murder grave that turns out to be a buried calf. Seein' the sheriff and Doc Doolie on the prairie in the dead of night—you ought to know that's when docs and sheriffs do a good part of their business. Diggin' up the New Boston graveyard . . . It's a wonder Olsen didn't lock you in the calaboose and throw away the key." He turned abruptly from Gault and said, "What's all this got to do with you, Wompler?"

Wompler's smile was as bland as a baby's. "Call it curiosity. Anything that affects the sheriff of Standard County, I take an interest in."

"How do you know the sheriff's affected?"

"I live in hope."

The two wills clashed like a meeting of swords. Gault expected to see Wompler give ground immediately; now he was surprised to see the silent struggle was on even terms. Wompler maintained his slack smile. Torgason's only sign of irritation was a slight narrowing of the eyes. "One of these days," he said flatly, "Olsen's goin' to get enough of you. And that will be the end of Harry Wompler."

"That," the former deputy sighed, "is a chance we all take, when we live in Standard County. Even you, Torgason. By the way," he added, "how'd you come to find us here?"

The detective looked woodenfaced. "A hand from headquarters joined Colton's brandin' crew. He said you and a stranger had been that way, and I decided to see what you was up to." Without warning, he grinned. It was a bizarre expression on that blank, brown face. "I figgered this is where I'd find you. At the Garnetts."

*

That afternoon Gault and Wompler pulled back from the farm and made camp again on the Little Wichita. From a distance they had scouted the farmyard and fields, without adding anything to their knowledge of the Garnetts. The young cowhand-cotton chopper had pulled out around midday. Shorty Pike had appeared from one of the barns and had gone to work in the vegetable garden near the house. A more peaceful scene would be difficult to imagine.

Shortly after the appearance of the posseman in the vegetable garden, Del Torgason had ridden south toward New Boston.

"Don't be fooled," Wompler warned. "He'll keep his eye on us. For the next few hours, anyway."

Gault scowled. "Why?"

"Because he's suspicious. It's his job."

As it had been Wirt Sewell's job, Gault thought wearily.

The moist, enervating electricity of springtime was in the air. "More rain," Wompler said sourly, eying the western sky. "Best see if we can find somethin' to get under."

The memory of the lanky express agent was still in Gault's mind. "The night I talked to Wirt Sewell, in the Garnett shed, he said he'd been layin' out somewhere. A shelf of some kind, along the riverbank."

"Whereabouts along the bank? It's a long river."

Gault tried to recall the agent's words. "I don't know that he said. But it couldn't have been far from the farm." They stood watching the thunderheads form in the west. Gault sighed wearily. The prospect of a cold soaking was not pleasant to think about. Without further discussion, the two men got saddled, pulled their stakepins and started back upstream.

The shelf was there, a big spearhead of limestone jutting out of the clay bank of the river. They staked the horses downstream and threw their beds beneath the rock roof. Not perfect, but a good deal better than no shelter at all.

Gault went through the futile motions of looking through his grub sack. It was empty. Wompler had never had any grub, only the bottle of whiskey from the Day and Night, and that had been emptied and discarded along the way. In the bottom of his saddle pocket Wompler found a piece of bone-hard jerky that some former New Boston livery customer had left. The two men divided the dried beef and hunkered down with their backs to the riverbank, cutting off small pieces with their pocketknives, working it between their teeth until it was soft enough to swallow.

"Life," the former deputy observed, "would be a good deal pleasanter if we had some coffee." He closed his eyes and dreamed for a moment. "Or whiskey."

The sun had fallen behind the bank of thunderheads. A steely grayness settled on the land, and there was no breath of movement in the air. The hush was so intense that they could hear each other breathing—or imagined that they could. "I'm beginnin' to wish," Wompler said to himself, "that I'd stayed where I was, back at the Day and Night." The reddish water of the Little Wichita shone dully, like sheet metal.

Suddenly the wind scent of ozone was in the air. In the distance there was a rustle of wind, faint but ominous. Wompler hunched his head down between his shoulders and groaned. "Here she comes!"

By common consent they had not built a fire. Without coffee, it hardly seemed worth the trouble. Anyway, they both felt more comfortable behind a cover of darkness. Gault buttoned his windbreaker to the throat, pulled his hat down firmly on his forehead and settled himself for a miserable night.

The first fat raindrop struck the river underbrush like a liquid bullet. Then there was another sound. Gault heard it, listened to it dully. Suddenly, with wrenching pain in his side, he lurched to his feet. "Somebody's after the horses!"

He grabbed the Winchester and jacked a cartridge into the chamber with one motion. Wompler already had his .45 in his hand. For a moment he was as taut as a finely tuned fiddle. Then, just as suddenly, he relaxed. "It's Torgason. I told you he'd be watchin' us."

The stock detective appeared in a stand of gaudy sumac. He bulled his way through the brush and ducked beneath the shelf as the first wave of the storm swept over them. Torgason, his saddle on his left shoulder, his rifle in his hand, stood looking at them with a wooden-faced stare. He eased the saddle to the ground but did not put aside the rifle. "I knowed you'd manage to find a soft place for yourself, Wompler. Don't mind if I set a while, do you?"

Wompler smiled his heatless smile. "Proud to have you. If you brought some coffee."

Thunder broke over their heads and rain fell in shimmering sheets. "Plenty of coffee," the detective told them. "Dry salt meat, and cornmeal, too. Now, if somebody thought to bring in some firewood before the rain started . . ."

Wompler groaned. Somehow the discomfort of their cold, damp cave was made even less appealing, knowing that hot trail fare was there within easy reach. If they could only have built a fire.

Torgason turned to Gault, and Gault met the detective's chilly stare with one of his own. "Seems like you didn't have much trouble finding us."

"Not much," Torgason rested his rifle on his saddle. "I've been watchin' you since we split up at the Garnett place."

"Would you mind tellin' us what makes us so interestin'?"

Torgason looked as if he might smile, but he didn't. "Wompler here's a suspected cattle rustler—that's always interestin' to a stock detective. And there's some things about you, too, Gault. A stranger lands in New Boston on the day Wolf Garnett's buried, bustin' full of questions that's none of his business. On top of everything else, by your own word, you killed a county official."

"A posseman."

"A paid official. As legal, according to county law, as the sheriff hisself."

"I didn't know you'd took to readin' law," Wompler said dryly.

Torgason ignored him. "You killed him," he said to Gault. "And the sheriff let you go. I find that interestin'."

Gault felt anger rising in his throat, but he choked it down. The old line rider had said that Torgason could help him, and he didn't want to fight with anyone who might be able to do that. Harry Wompler regarded the two with a loose smile and seemed totally undisturbed. "Don't mind Torgason," he said lazily. "He likes to get folks riled. In the hopes they'll spout somethin' he can hang them with later."

More thunder rumbled in the darkness. Beyond the shelf the rain was driving down like silver spikes.

Wompler yawned. "If you boys can stand the loss of my company, I think I'll catch myself some sleep." He untied his roll and threw it on the ground next to the river-bank.

Gault and the detective sat with their backs to the rock, staring out at the storm. "How'd you come to get tied up with Wompler?" Torgason asked when the silence became uncomfortable.

"Same way I heard about you. Yorty told me about him."

"That old man," Torgason said coldly, "has got a big mouth."

For some time the two men crouched in uncomfortable silence. Between gusting attacks of the storm they could hear Wompler snoring. When Torgason finally decided to speak, his tone was controlled and thoughtful. "I've been thinkin'. It must of been on a night like this that you talked to Wirt Sewell."

"Just about. But darker."

"And again when you heard what you thought was a shot."

"That was a dream—about the storm, anyway." Gault studied him cautiously. "Why do you ask?"

"Like Wompler said, it's my job to be suspicious."

For some time they crouched silently, watching the storm. Then Torgason said abruptly, "Tell me again about Colly Fay. The things you found in his saddle pocket."

Gault had already gone over this part of the story, but apparently Torgason was still unsatisfied. Patiently, Gault collected his thoughts and prepared to cover the ground again. "There was the ring, the one I gave to my wife. I told you about that." Torgason, a crouching shadow backlighted by sheet lightning, nodded. Gault went on. "There were six double-eagles, and some other coins. A roll of greenbacks wrapped in oilskin. A silver pocketknife, the kind a city dude might carry for cuttin' cigars. Woman's earrings, set with glassy sparkles. Maybe diamonds. A string of milk-colored beads that might have been pearls."

"Is that all?"

Gault drove his memory back to that bitter moment when he had opened the little buckskin pouch and found the ring. "No, there was a watch."

The big-shouldered shadow cocked its head thoughtfully. "What about the watch?"

Gault could see it lying there on the dirty flannel shirt, surrounded by Colly's other items of loot. "It was gold—yellow gold—stem-wound, with a gold face cover. There was a heavy gold chain that must of cost the owner plenty, if it was real gold. There was some writing—engraving—on the face cover."

Torgason's shadow came almost rigidly erect. "What did it say?"

"It was foreign writin' of some kind; I couldn't read it." He thought for a moment. "Somethin' about a fort."

Wompler, who had been snoring only a moment before, sat up on his blanket and said, "*Fortes fortuna juvat.*"

And Torgason said—with something like a drawn-out sigh—"General Mallard Springfield Heath." He lurched to his feet and stared out at the night. The rain was still coming down. "What," he asked in a curiously flat tone, "did the sheriff say when he saw that watch?"

"Olsen?" Gault tried to think back to the moment when he had dumped the parcel on the sheriff's table. "Nothin' special that I recollect. He just looked at it and wanted to know where I got it. Look here," he said, irritated by the air of mystery that had suddenly built up inside the cave, "what's this about forts and generals? What do they have to do with Colly Fay and the sheriff?"

"Not forts," Wompler drawled with the dry superiority of the half-educated. "Fortes fortuna juvat. 'Fortune favors the brave.' The motto of General Heath's cavalry regiment, when he was a colonel. Before he was promoted to general and got hisself killed."

Torgason turned to Gault and asked sharply. "You never heard of General Mallard Heath?"

Gault glanced from one dark, tense figure to the other. "No, I never heard of him. I guess maybe it's time I did."

CHAPTER EIGHT

Torgason had turned back to the storm and was glaring out at the slanting rain. Harry Wompler undertook to enlighten Gault on the life and death of General Mallard Springfield Heath. "The *late* General Mallard Springfield Heath," he said, with his slack smile.

Heath was a Texas man, born and raised in the brush country along the Nueces, although few Texans would admit to him since the war. Mallard Heath was one of those rare patriots—or traitors, depending on who was telling it —who abandoned his cow-hunting operations in Texas, ignoring the call of Hood and other Southerners, to throw in his lot with the Yankees.

It had been a wise and profitable decision—up to a point. He rose from the ranks and at the end of the war wore the eagle of a Union colonel on his shoulders. Wisely, he declined to return to Texas, except in line of duty and always in uniform. It was in the performance of such duty, in 1878, that General Heath personally oversaw the shipment of $200,000 in gold bullion from Fort Belknap, Texas, to Camp Supply, in the Indian Territory. And it was somewhere between these two points, in the foothills of the Wichitas, that the escort was ambushed, officers and troopers killed to a man, the gold vanished . . .

"Without a trace," Wompler finished in some excitement. "There's been Army men, and U.D. deputies, and all kinds of sharpshooters and highbinders lookin' for that gold. Never a trace. Mexican and U.S. troops have been watchin' the Bravo for eight years. Same up north on the Canadian line. Never a clue." He chuckled dryly. "Then one day a Territory cowman named Gault walks into Olsen's office and turns over old *Fortes fortuna juvat's* pocketwatch. And what does the sheriff do when he sees that watch? He don't do nothin'. Torgason, *that's* somethin' *I* find interestin'."

The stock detective glared at the rain and made no comment. "Picture it in your mind, Gault," Wompler was saying gleefully. "You took that watch off of the handpicked posseman of Olsen's handpicked deputy. I wish I could see the sheriff's face when he tries to explain that to the county judge. Squirmin' like a city dude with saddle galls. I've waited a long time to see that."

"You may have some waitin' to do yet," Torgason said sourly.

But Wompler only chuckled. "You're just mad because you never thought of it before now. Olsen and Wolf Garnett in cahoots all this time, and nobody guessin' a thing! Don't feel bad about it, Torgason, I never guessed it either. Like everybody else, I figgered the sheriff and Esther . . ."

Torgason turned from the mouth of the cave. "Whiskey's made your brain soft, Wompler. I don't say that Olsen ain't got his faults, but he wouldn't throw in with a killer like Wolf Garnett."

Almost gaily Wompler waved the objection away. "Might be surprisin' what *any* of us would do, if there was an army wagon full of gold in the balance." That thought had a quieting effect on Torgason, but Wompler went on with his dreaming. "Yes sir, nearly a quarter of a million dollars is a lot of money. Think about it! We'd all be rich as hog fat if we could find out where it's hid. And we might even find out what happened to Wirt Sewell."

Torgason sounded indignant. "How could a stolen gold shipment have anything to do with Sewell?"

"Maybe his suspicious ways got him on the track of it—and Wolf killed him."

"Wolf Garnett's dead."

"Anyhow, that's what Olsen wants everybody to believe."

The rain was beginning to slacken as the storm moved on to the east. The men in the shallow cave sniffed the wet, clean smell of a washed earth. Within a matter of minutes the rain stopped completely. The thunder was a distant rumble, the lightning as delicate as foxfire on the far horizon. They could hear the rushing and splashing as water from a dozen flooded gullies and arroyos dumped into the river.

"It's all over," Torgason announced unnecessarily. Hurrying clouds slipped over the prairie, revealing a pale, cold moon, and stars that glittered like swordpoints.

Wompler had fallen into a strange silence. He sat hunched over, his back to the clay riverbank, smoking one of his poorly made sputtering cigarettes. Suddenly he got to his feet and began rolling his blanket.

"What do you think you're doin'?" Torgason demanded.

"Somethin's been botherin' me all day and I couldn't put a finger on it. But thinkin' about Wirt Sewell brought it back again—it's that calf that's buried in the wash back of the Garnett house."

Gault got to his feet. "What about it?"

"I'm not sure. But I aim to find out."

Torgason, who had been standing in the wet weeds beyond the shelf, came back into the cavelike darkness and said, with undisguised contempt, "In the middle of the night, and a wet one at that? Wompler, you're loco."

The former deputy looked at him with a dark grin and continued tying his bedroll.

Gault stood for a moment, thinking about the day and what had happened. In the back of his mind that calf had bothered him too. As Wompler ducked out of the cave carrying his bed and saddle, Gault said, "Bring the horses up here. I'll go with you."

Torgason sighed. It was a long-suffering sound of a reasonable man condemned to deal eternally with fools. "What you expect to find on a dark and boggy prairie, in the middle of the night, I don't know. But you might as well bring my horse too."

*

The horses plodded heavily over the spongy sod along the river. The men rode northward along the crest of the riverbottom, and soon they could see the field of young cotton, and the smaller one of corn, spread out below them, the neat rows standing in water and silvery in the moonlight.

The arroyo where they had found the calf lay like an open wound behind the farmhouse, slanting southward to the river. The house stood dark and sullen on the unfenced ground, but in one of the larger outbuildings, which Gault knew to be the main barn, the reddish light of a coal oil lantern shone through the cracks around the door.

The horsebackers reined up and studied the light. "What do you make of it?" Wompler asked at last.

"Shorty Pike," Gault said, more concerned with the arroyo than the barn. "Most likely that's where he throws his bed."

The wet clay walls of the gully glistened in the moonlight, but most of the water had already rushed headlong into the river. The riders got down and led their animals along the wash. Gault was the first to see what they were looking for. "This is where the calf was buried."

Wompler grounded his reins and eased himself down the slick wall of the arroyo. "This is it. Not much of a burial job, whoever done it. The calf's almost washed out."

He grunted several times and swore to himself. "Wait till I light a match."

A match flared on Wompler's thumbnail, and for an instant the floodswept bottom of the wash, the dead calf, and part of what lay beneath the calf, were etched with steelpoint sharpness. Wompler pulled away from that shallow grave, his face looking white and drawn in the sulphurish light. Then the match went out.

"Give me a hand, somebody."

Gault and Torgason slid down to the muddy bottom of the arroyo. They had seen what Wompler had seen, but they did not completely believe it. "Grab one of the forelegs," Wompler said with unaccustomed authority. "We'll have to get the calf out of the hole before we can be sure of anything."

Gault grabbed a foreleg and Torgason and Wompler took the hind quarters and pulled the animal out of the hole. With great care, Wompler dried his hands on the seat of his pants, then struck another match. Once again, by the light of that tiny sulphur fire, they looked into the grave. The dead eyes of Wirt Sewell looked back at them.

The three men seemed to breathe together. In and out. Then Wompler spoke. "Now I think I'd like to see about that light in the Garnett barn."

"Later," Torgason said quietly. "After we attend to Sewell."

"There ain't nothin' we can do for him."

They looked at one another, two men surprisingly equal now, and strong willed. Not dedicated enemies, exactly, but not friends, either. "First," Torgason said again in the same quiet tone, "we'll attend to Sewell."

Gault avoided further argument by climbing out of the wash and stripping his own bedroll of its tarpaulin cover. "Pass him up here. We'll cover him up and lay him out somewhere, out of the weather. The rest will have to wait till later."

After a moment's hesitation the two men in the wash nodded together. With gentleness that might have been surprising to some, they lifted the body out of the hole and passed it up to Gault who covered it with his tarp.

As if motivated by a single mind, the three men wrapped the body in its canvas shroud and tied it on behind Wompler's saddle, because Wompler was the lightest of the three men and his rented gelding was the most docile of the animals. "Now," Gault said stiffly, "I think it's time we saw about that light."

But first they tied their horses at one of the small sheds and laid the express agent's body out on the straw-covered floor. The three men looked at one another and Wompler asked dryly, "Is there anything anybody wants to say?"

What was there to say? The shot that Gault thought he had heard—he had heard. Sewell had put his hawkish nose into a place where it wasn't welcome. And someone had killed him. And buried him. And then, as an added safety measure, they had killed a calf to fill the grave, in case somebody found it. But they hadn't counted on a flash flood.

"Why would they bury Sewell in a wash so close to the house?" Wompler asked.

And Torgason answered softly and calmly, having thought it all out beforehand. "Because it was handy. An easy place to dig. And because they didn't care about makin' a good job of it, because they didn't figger to be around when he was found. If he was found." He started to build a cigarette, but his hands were not quite steady and he tore the paper. He put the makings away in disgust. "Then somebody got worried and decided to hide the body with the calf." He nodded to himself. "It wasn't a bad notion. If it hadn't been for the storm."

Gault was seeing the posseman's face as he came out of the wash that morning with the shovel. "Shorty Pike," he said.

"That's what I aim to find out." The stock detective smiled coldly at Wompler and Gault. "If you gents want to come along, that's all right with me."

They circled wide around the sheds, keeping out of sight of the house. Torgason and Wompler arrived at the barn well ahead of Gault. His side was beginning to hurt again; his breathing was ragged. Torgason looked at him. "You all right?"

Gault nodded, sagging against the side of the barn until he recovered his breath. Then they moved to the double plank door and Wompler said, "Stand back out of the light when I open it." Quietly, Gault and Torgason levered cartridges into their rifles.

No sound came from inside the barn. Well, Gault reasoned, it was well past bedtime, they were probably sleeping.

With the lantern burning? "Open it," he told Wompler. The former deputy set himself, then suddenly flung the doors wide and dived for darkness. Torgason and Gault snapped their rifles to their shoulders. Nothing happened. No sound, no movement. After a moment Gault edged around one side of the door, Torgason around the other. Behind them, somewhere in the darkness, they could hear Wompler breathing. There was no one in the barn.

Without turning his head, Gault snapped to Wompler, "Keep an eye on the house and the other sheds." Then he and Torgason made an inspection of the barn. On the pole rack that served as a hay loft they found an area of packed hay where someone had been bedding down. But there was no sign of occupation now. Gault eased himself down on the hay platform and held his side. Torgason eased his Winchester hammer to half cock and called to Wompler. "Anything movin' out there?"

"Quiet as a graveyard," Wompler called from the gaping doorway.

Gault shoved himself to his feet. "I want to see the house."

Esther Garnett was not in the house. No one was. The three men stationed themselves as they had at the barn. Wompler pounded on the door several times. Then Gault stepped forward and kicked the door open.

"Miss Garnett?"

A muslin curtain sighed at one of the front windows. Nothing else moved. Gault felt along his hatband, found a match and lit a coal oil lamp. Wompler, who in better times had been in this house as a guest, stepped inside and made a sound of surprise as he stared around at the blank walls. "There used to be pictures over there . . ." He pointed. "Of Esther's ma and pa. And there was other things, too . . ."

Gault moved across the room to a closed door and kicked it open. It was a bedroom—black oak dresser, washstand, bed. But the bed had been stripped, the drawers of the dresser pulled out and emptied.

He moved to the kitchen where the iron cookstove was in place, and several pots and pans, but most of the dishes had been taken from the upright kitchen safe. Wompler came to the doorway and stood there, his face puzzled. "Esther set great store in them dishes. Her grandma brought them from across the water, she told me once."

"Look at this," Torgason called from another part of the house. Gault followed the voice to a small, boxed-in porch, sometimes called a sleeping porch. What had caught Torgason's attention was a rude knock-up bunk, a thing of blackjack poles and haywire, strung with frayed well-rope. More interesting than the bed, which might have been accounted for, was the litter of burnt matches and brownpaper cigarette butts on the floor.

The three men studied the room, sized it up in their minds, but did not discuss it at the moment. "Probably a waste of time," Torgason said finally, "but we might as well see if there's anything in the sheds."

They found a heavy breaking plow, almost new, and

other farm tools. But no wagon, and only odds and ends of harness. The milk cow had been turned out; the mule was gone. At last they returned to the house where Wompler's instinct led him to a fruitjar half full of clear whiskey, tucked away beneath the rope-strung bunk.

Gault and Wompler sat at the cooktable, which was still in place. Torgason stood in the doorway glaring at the box walls of the sleeping porch. Wompler drank deeply of the raw liquor and passed it to Gault, who tasted it, but Torgason would not touch it. "Wompler, you and Miss Garnett was thick once, they say. What do you make of this?"

The whiskey worked rapidly on Wompler's taut nerves. He sagged in the chair, his eyes going slightly glassy. "She's pulled out. That's clear enough, ain't it?"

"Why?" the stock detective demanded.

Wompler had another go at the fruitjar. "I don't know. It's been a long spell since Esther and me . . ." He sighed and smiled his crooked smile. "Pulled out, that's all there is to it. Took the wagon, the mule, the dishes, a few other things."

"How about this bunk on the sleepin' porch."

This was the thing that disturbed them. More than the missing mule and wagon; more, even, than Esther Garnett's disappearance. Esther was what was known as a "decent" woman; none of them had any doubts on this point. But that extra bunk, and the whiskey, and the litter of cigarettes and matches . . . Even in Gault's mind it made a jarring picture.

"Shorty Pike?" Torgason asked at last.

Wompler snorted. "A highbinder like Shorty, sleepin' in the same house with Esther Garnett?" he grinned loosely to show that the idea was ridiculous.

Gault had an idea that wasn't so ridiculous.

"Wolf Garnett," he said.

They stared at him. "Once," Wompler said, after a long silence, "I knowed an old galoot that got hisself in a scrap with a band of Kiowas. They killed his woman and his two boys, and then they strung him up over a torture fire and would of cooked him like a fat dog, except some horse soldiers from Belknap happened along before they finished him. From that time on, that old geezer seen Kiowas everywhere he looked. Behind every manure pile and fire-barrel, a Kiowa. Around every bend, behind every tree. Kiowa." The former deputy took a long drink from the fruitjar. "That's the way you are, Gault. Everywhere you look, there's Wolf Garnett."

"Then who's been sleepin' on that bunk? Sleepin', smokin', and drinkin' clear corn whiskey?"

Wompler was silent for several moments. "Wolf," he said at last, "is dead. Everything points to it. Still," he went on thoughtfully, "if he *wasn't* dead, and if this *is* the bunk where he's been sleepin', it would clear up a lot of things in my mind. It would explain why Esther all of a sudden didn't want me on the place. It would explain why Olsen drummed up that rustlin' story and then fired me."

From the doorway Torgason looked at the former deputy and said, "Comes mornin' we'll know more about it. Just as soon as it's light enough to track that wagon."

＊

The tracks, for a way, were easy enough to follow, but the trace became confused when it crossed and mingled with other wagon tracks on the stage road to Gainsville. Then, on a bed of gravel and shale, they lost all sign. The storm had washed it away, erased it from the prairie.

But there was a few things they had learned. One, the wagon was being drawn by two animals. They concluded, without discussing the matter, that Shorty Pike's horse had been put in harness with the Garnett mule. Also, it was now clear that Esther Garnett's destination was generally north from the Little Wichita, although she seemed to be taking a roundabout way of getting there—wherever it was. It occurred to the three men, almost at the same time, that she was carefully avoiding all steep slopes or grades, preferring to go farther and keep to flatter ground.

The same thought was in all their minds, but Gault was the one to voice it. "Gold, they say, is right heavy. I don't know how much $200,000 would weigh, but I don't expect I'd want to put a two-horse team up any steep grades if I was haulin' it."

Around midday they unbitted the horses, chewed some jerky and made coffee from Torgason's meager supplies. Wompler and the detective were strangely quiet. Sudden visions of wealth rose up like walls of gold and isolated them.

It was Wompler, with the honesty of a man who had nothing to lose, who finally voiced his thoughts. "I always wondered what it would be like to be rich. Maybe we'll all find out, before this little set-to is over."

"We don't *know* she's got any gold in that wagon," Gault said.

"I got a feelin'," Wompler said comfortably. "It's the only thing that makes sense. The way she's drivin' that wagon. General Heath's gold watch. Where would Colly get his hands on that watch if he hadn't been with the bunch that bushwhacked the escort? And Wolf's bunch is the only one he ever ran with." The ex-deputy smiled. His eyes had a faraway look. "We're on the track of that gold, all right. If it ain't in the wagon, then Wolf hid it somewheres. Either way, all we have to do is stay on the job, and Esther Garnett will lead us to it."

"Maybe," Del Torgason said dryly. "But the sheriff has seen that watch too. If there's any gold, he knows as much about it as we do."

They pulled their stakepins and continued to the north. As the mild spring sun slipped away to the west they spotted the two horsebackers moving over the sandhills along the north bank of the Red. "Colton," Torgason said with some surprise.

"And the old line rider, Elbert Yorty."

Gault studied them carefully. He easily recognized the old cowhand. The other man was a thick-set, heavy rider, one whose rocklike weight would punish even the strongest saddle animal. This was Gault's first look at the manager of the Circle-R.

"Let's talk to them," Wompler said. "Maybe one of them caught sight of the wagon."

The three men put their horses down the long grade toward the sandy banks of the Red. At first it appeared that Colton was going to pretend that he hadn't seen them; he and Yorty reined their animals toward a thicket of budding trees. Suddenly Wompler rose in his saddle and bellowed, "Hold up there, Colton!" Then, with a grin at his two companions, he said amiably, "Even if I ain't a deputy any more, I can holler like one."

It was effective. The ranch manager pulled up with a jerk. After a hurried conversation between the old line rider and his boss, Yorty headed west toward the line camp and Colton reluctantly pointed up the long slope.

"I figgered," Torgason told the manager, "you'd still be out seein' that the crew got all the strays branded."

Colton smiled wanly. "I got good hands; they tend to business without me watchin' over them all the time."

Torgason started to say something, but Wompler butted in. "You or your boys see anything of a wagon movin' up this way from the south?"

Colton looked at Wompler as if he were seeing him for the first time. "What kind of wagon?"

"Light spring rig; farm wagon. Had the sheet up, most likely."

The rancher shook his head slowly. "Nope, we never saw any kind of rig like that."

Gault was puzzled to see Torgason quietly fold his hands

on the saddle horn, with the bored air of a man who had no personal interest in the proceedings. "Much obliged, anyhow," he said. "Nothin' to fret about—it ain't important."

Colton, with a look of relief on his face, started to rein toward Circle-R headquarters. At the last moment Gault reached out and caught his animal by the head stall. "Just a minute, Colton. There's somethin' I've been aimin' to ask you about, but I never got the chance before now. You recollect back several nights ago—there was a thunderstorm—that Doc Doolie was out at your headquarters patchin' up one of your men?"

The ranch manager turned to Gault and looked blank. "The doc hasn't been near my headquarters in over a year."

Gault smiled without warmth. "That's all I wanted to know."

Once again Colton reined away from them. Wompler, glaring at the rancher's back, said, "He was lyin' about not seein' the wagon—it was all over his face."

"Most likely," Torgason shrugged. "But you can't get a straight answer from a straw boss. If we want the truth about what they seen or what they didn't see, we'll have to talk to Yorty."

Gault was beginning to understand Torgason's reasoning. "Because," he said, "Yorty's an old man and scared of losin' his job? He'd be scared *not* to tell the truth, to a stock detective."

Torgason smiled coolly. "You're learnin', Gault.

CHAPTER NINE

They found the old line rider hurriedly rolling his bed in front of his half-dugout hut. There was dismay, and maybe a little fear, in his eyes when he saw the three horse-backers coming toward him.

"Aimin' on takin' a trip, Yorty?" Torgason asked, smiling his smile so thin and heatless that it was almost a smirk.

The old man's gaze darted from Gault to Torgason to Wompler. "Not a trip. There's a outbreak of colic over on the west pasture that the boss wants me to see about."

"Fine." The detective honed his knife-edged smile. "Proud to see an old hand lookin' after his job." The words "old hand" had not been wasted on Elbert Yorty. His face became a little longer, his eyes a little paler. No one had to point out to him that a word from an Association man could get even the most competent cowhand fired without notice or explanation. With that unpleasantry behind him, Torgason softened a little. "What we want to know, Yorty, is about the wagon."

The old man seemed to sigh. "The spring rig? Farm wagon, from the looks of it, with the sheet up?"

"That's the one."

Wompler shot a glance at Gault and smiled crookedly.

He had used this same technique on the old wrangler at Circle-R headquarters.

The line rider shrugged and spread his hands in an attitude of surrender. "Come across the prairie first thing this mornin', headin' west along the river. I figgered it was headin' for the old Indian crossin' about a mile upstream, but I didn't foller to make sure."

Gault leaned over his saddle horn. "Who was drivin'?"

"Kind of squarebuilt bird, not too tall. I think it was Shorty Pike."

"Anybody else?"

"That's all I seen. But like I said, the sheet was up. Could of been somebody under it, I guess." He paused for a moment, trying to remember. "Nope, that's all. Just the stubby-lookin' galoot up on the box, that might of been Shorty Pike. A black mule and a chestnut stud was in the traces."

Wompler broke in impatiently. "Why didn't you want to tell us about this?"

"Boss told me not to."

"Why wouldn't Colton want you to tell us about the wagon?"

The old man smiled sadly. "Not so long ago—around dinnertime, I guess it was—the sheriff and that young sprout of a deputy, they come up to our camp and asked about that wagon, just the way you're askin' now."

Gault came suddenly erect. Torgason looked surprised. But Wompler only smiled his slack smile and grunted. "The sheriff told you and Colton not to say anything about seein' the wagon."

"That's the way it was."

Scowling, Gault turned this information in his mind. "Is that all?" Wompler asked.

"Just about. The sheriff said him and the deputy seen some Circle-R strays as they was comin' from headquarters. He didn't put it in so many words, but it was easy to get the feelin' that it might be a good notion for us to pull away from the river and work the brandin' crew back south for a day or so. That's what Colton was doin' when you found us."

"Does Colton take orders on ranch business from the sheriff?"

"When the sheriff is Grady Olsen, he does."

Torgason laughed quietly. "You better see about that outbreak of colic," he told the old man, with as much gentleness as he could manage. But it was too late for gentleness, as far as Elbert Yorty was concerned. The fear of old age was in his bones.

*

Gault and Torgason and Wompler rode upstream, with Wompler taking the lead. The greedy light of gold was in the former deputy's eyes. Torgason, despite a conscious effort to stay disinterested, allowed his wooden mask to slip from time to time. Even Gault, whose obsession was revenge, not riches, could not escape the fascination of $200,000.

"What do you make of it?" Gault asked the stock detective. "About the sheriff and the deputy showing up here, so far from New Boston?"

"The sheriff," Torgason said dryly, "don't let hisself get hemmed in much by county lines. State lines neither, for that matter." He shrugged and smiled his brittle smile. "When Olsen seen that watch, I figger he started thinkin' just the way we did. About that army gold. And he aims to get it."

"Wompler tells me that Olsen is in love with Esther Garnett."

The stock detective looked as if he might be laughing on the inside, though his wooden face never changed expression. "Our Sheriff Olsen is a sensible man. He knows he could buy a whole pack of women, maybe some of them even better lookin' than Esther Garnett, for almost a quarter of a million dollars."

It was Wompler who saw the wagon first. The three men reined up sharply and studied it for some time without speaking.

The driver, apparently, had lost control of the wagon before it had ever reached the rock crossing. It had skidded off the near bank, plunging off the shoulder of sand and landing in one of the shallow channels on the Texas side of the river. There it lay now, on its side, the bows shattered, the dirty white sheet trailing in the reddish water. Several yards from the wagon a broken wheel was partially imbedded in the sand. There was no team.

"Like Gault says," Wompler said excitedly, "that gold's heavy stuff. She couldn't of took it with her. It must still be in the wagon."

"We don't know there was ever any gold in the wagon," Gault reminded him.

But Wompler was already spurring his horse down the sandy embankment. The former lawman swung out of his saddle and clambered into the half-submerged wagon box. After a moment his head appeared over the sideboards. "Everything's a mess in here. Get a loop on this wagon box and pull it right-side up, then we'll see where we stand."

Obediently, Torgason and Gault tied onto the submerged bow brackets, then backed their horses in the shallow water and pulled the wagon upright. Wompler scrambled back inside and began tearing away what remained of the canvas sheet.

Esther Garnett's prized china dishes lay shattered in the bottom of the wagon. A bundle of clothing had broken open and odds and ends of female attire floated on the dirty water. What appeared to be a bedroll was wedged in mud beneath the driver's seat. If there had ever been any gold in the wagon, it was not there now.

Wompler stared at the waste of useless articles floating in the wagon box. His face was crumpled in disappointment, and for one uneasy moment Gault thought he might break into tears. "There ain't nothin' here!" he exploded. He grabbed up an unbroken plate and smashed it against the sideboards. "No gold! Nothin' at all!"

Torgason put his sturdy claybank into deeper water and slowly circled the wagon. He leaned over in the saddle, looking intently at something beneath the front wheels. "Not quite nothin'," he said without expression. "Here's Shorty Pike."

The stock detective eased the claybank against the front of the wagon box and rocked it gently in the shallow water. The body of the stocky posseman came to the surface, floating face up, the wide eyes staring unblinkingly at the blue spring sky.

Wompler made a whistling sound as he sucked in his breath. He stared over the side of the wagon. "Has he been shot?"

"Can't tell," Torgason said matter of factly. He shook out his loop and expertly caught one of the corpse's feet and dragged it onto the sandy beach. With cool competence, the detective got down, turned the body over and examined it. "He wasn't shot," he said at last. "He didn't need it." He pointed to the saucerlike dent in the back of Shorty's head. "Pitched out when the wagon went off the bank. Hit a rock, maybe. Whatever it was, he never knowed what hit him." With a faintly surprisingly show of delicacy, he closed the dead man's eyes.

Wompler's eyes widened in alarm. "Maybe somethin' happened to Esther, too."

"Maybe the sheriff and his deputy," Gault offered.

Torgason nodded but made no comment. They put their horses across the river and picked up some tracks on the north bank. "But whose tracks are they?" Wompler asked. "Esther, or Olsen and Finley?"

Gault rode up to the crest of sandhills that lined the north bank of the Red. "What're you lookin' for?" Wompler wanted to know.

"The mule that was in the traces with Shorty's animal. It don't make sense that she'd hang onto that mule when she had a perfectly good saddle horse to ride."

Wompler had a bright idea. "Maybe that's what happened to the gold. She packed it on the mule."

Torgason regarded him with contempt. In the back of Gault's mind he heard the two men bickering angrily, but his thoughts were somewhere else. He rode along the collar of the sandhills and picked up more tracks, but again it was impossible to say whose they were.

Lord, Gault thought wearily, I feel like I've been traveling half a lifetime. Without sleep or rest. Sometimes he almost forgot why he was doing it. There were even times when the face of Wolf Garnett became mingled with other faces in his memory. "It's because I'm tired, Martha," he said aloud. "It ain't that I'm forgetting. It ain't that I've got any notion of lettin' it rest—you can depend on that." He looked up to see Torgason and Wompler staring at him strangely.

They pressed on to the north, following what may or may not have been trail left by Esther Garnett.

They were in Comanche country now, somewhere below the west branch of Cashe Creek which, in places, was more of a river than the Red. They crossed one of the many small streams that fingered out from the west branch. They were now in a country of gentle green hills and valleys, country that would one day be rich farmland but was now leased pasture.

Suddenly Wompler came up in his stirrups and said, "What's that?" He pointed to a small piece of broken ground in the valley below. The crooked rows of poorly planted corn could only mean that the Quaker Indian agents had converted a Comanche to farming.

Gault told them that it was an Indian farm, and Torgason said quickly, "You used to run cattle in this country. Talk to the Indian, ask if he's seen anything of a white woman horsebackin' it this way."

Gault shrugged. "If I remember any Comanche."

The Indian's name was Watch Horses and he was a Quahada Comanche which, according to white horse soldiers, made him one of the best light cavalryman in the world. But not any more. His people were beaten, scattered, and there was defeat in his dark Indian eyes as he leaned on his hoe and looked up at Gault.

With the aid of sign and a few words of Comanche, Gault asked if a woman horsebacker had passed this way.

Watch Horses said that his wife had gone to the Indian agency that morning to trade some skins. "No," Gault corrected himself. "*To'savit*. White woman."

Watch Horses considered for a moment. It was possible, he said at last, that a white woman had passed this way. But he had not seen her.

"Did he see Olsen and Finley?" Torgason asked.

Gault relayed the question, and Watch Horses shrugged. Yes, two white men passed this way not long ago, heading north. But nowdays Indianland was overrun with white cowmen; the Quahada had not paid them any particular attention.

"Let's go," Wompler said impatiently. "It was Olsen and Finley. I can feel it in my bones."

This time they did not bother with tracks, they struck due north, in the direction indicated by the old Comanche. There was an electric urgency in the air. For Torgason and Wompler it was the prospect of sudden riches. For Gault it was something more insidious; there were times when he thought it was madness. A man *must* be loco, he told himself, to spend the best part of a year chasing after ghosts . . . But then he would see that stagecoach going off the mountain road, and Martha's eyes wide with terror. Loco or not, he could not stop now.

They topped one of those many grassy hillocks that punctuated the flat prairie between the Wichitas and the Red. Torgason, riding a little ahead of the others, raised one hand. With a nod he indicated a distant stream, a small creek clearly defined by the lacy green of budding timber. "A little to the right of the tallest cottonwood. Tell me what you see."

Squinting, Gault and Wompler leaned forward in their saddles. Gault shook his head. "I don't see anything." Wompler grunted, indicating that he didn't either.

Torgason scratched the bristling beard on his chin. "Maybe it was nothin'. A flash of light. Sunlight hittin' a piece of mica, maybe."

"Or gunsteel?" Gault asked.

". . . We'll see."

They spread out as they started down the slope to the creek, spacing themselves out, making the target less tempting. They moved to within two hundred yards of the cottonwood—easy rifle range. Still there was nothing to be seen.

Gault turned in his saddle to look at the detective. Torgason was again scratching his chin in an unconscious show of concern. He made pushing motions with his hands, telling Gault and Wompler that they would approach the cottonwood from different directions. It was then that Torgason's horse fell.

Gault heard the animal grunt—then he heard the report of the rifle. The sturdy claybank stumbled, tossed its head in a moment of wildness, and pitched to the near side. Torgason was grabbing for his own rifle and trying to free his right foot from the stirrup when the horse crashed on top of him.

Acting on his cowman's instinct, Gault ignored for the moment the danger from the creekbank. He grabbed his

Winchester, dumped out of the saddle and raced to Torgason's aid. Wompler obeying his own instincts, ignored Torgason and spurred to the bottom of the slope, which put him below the rifleman's line of sight.

"Don't be a fool!" Torgason grated. "My leg's busted. I can't move. Get away from this hilltop before that rifleman finishes both of us."

The distant rifle barked twice, as if in anger. Gault dived for the ground as the two bullets seared the air over his head. Using the dead horse as a breastworks, Gault said, "I'll try to get the weight off of you. When you're clear, haul yourself back out of the way."

The rifle barked again; this time the bullet slammed into the dead horse with a sickening thud. Gault got his shoulder beneath the cantle of the saddle and lifted with all his strength. Grunting with pain, Torgason pulled himself up to a sitting position, freed his foot from the stirrup and crawled back from the dead animal.

The detective lay on the springy sod, panting shallowly, great beads of sweat on his forehead. "What happened to Wompler?" he asked at last.

"Spurred to the bottom of the slope where the rifleman can't see him."

Torgason smiled grimly. "He ain't as big a fool as I thought." He panted some more and wiped his forehead. "I don't reckon you got a look at whoever's doin' the shootin'?"

"They're hid back in the timber along the creekbank." A bullet plowed into the ground alongside the dead horse. "It must be the sheriff." Gault eased his head over the edge of the saddle and saw Wompler waving to him from the bottom of the slope. "Wompler's signalin'. I better see what he wants."

"And get yourself shot for your trouble?"

"I think he wants us to split up and see if we can get the creekbank in a crossfire."

"Listen to Wompler and he'll get you killed." The detective sighed and lay back and stared up at the dazzling sky. "On the other hand, if Olsen aims to finish us, he'll finish us. It don't matter much what we do."

Gault considered for a moment. "From what I seen of Olsen, he didn't strike me as a murderer."

"Gold makes men do funny things," Torgason said softly, still looking at the sky. "Gold and woman."

Gault snaked his arm around the claybank's shoulder and eased the saddle rifle out of the boot. He checked it quickly and put it in Torgason's hands. "Stay down out of sight. I'll come back soon's I can."

Before Torgason could speak, Gault lunged to his feet and began zigzagging down the grassy slope.

*

Wompler was waiting at the bottom, grinning his slack grin. "You're faster'n you look." Then he nodded toward the distant creek. "How does it look from the top of the hill?"

"Quiet. Maybe they pulled out."

"Or waitin' for us to come in closer so they can finish us off." Wompler made a wry face. "I sure would hate to blunder out there and get myself killed—with all that gold somewheres, just waitin' for us to come along and pick it up." Then, thoughtfully, "You game to circle around this knoll and see if we can find them?"

"And if we do find them?"

"We kill them," Wompler said matter of factly. He mounted his rented gelding, rode down the shallow valley to where Gault's buckskin was grazing. With an expert flip of his loop, he caught the buckskin and brought it back.

"What do you mean," Gault asked, taking the reins, "we kill them?"

Wompler looked surprised that anyone would be stupid

enough to ask such a question. "Two fewer ways we'll have to divide up the gold, when we find it."

"And what about Esther Garnett? Do we kill her, too?"

Wompler's expression turned wooden. "Esther Garnett's my business, Gault. You remember that and we'll get along fine."

✿

Gault rode cautiously south along the shallow depression between the two knolls; Wompler headed north. When a distance of several hundred yards separated them, they bore in toward the tall cottonwood where the riflefire had come from. All in all, it had taken the best part of an hour to get into position. The rifleman was gone.

They explored the area around the cottonwood. "Three horses, I make it," Wompler said, studying the tracks. "Shorty's chestnut, most likely, that Esther's ridin'. And Olsen's and Finley's animals." He straightened up, scowling. "And some barefoot tracks that probably belong to the Garnett mule. Wonder what they're draggin' that mule around for?"

Gault had discovered something that he found more interesting than the tracks of mules and horses. Beneath the cottonwood he carefully collected a half dozen burnt-out stubs of brownpaper cigarettes, and several broken sulphur matches. The last time he had seen this kind of litter it had been on the floor of Esther Garnett's sleeping porch.

"They're in a hurry," Wompler said unhappily. "Olsen's a careful worker—ordinarily he'd of set a trap for us and then laid back and wait for us to walk into it. But this is no ordinary time. He's in a hurry to get to that gold."

"We still don't know there *is* any gold. All we've got to go on is that watch that I found on Colly Fay."

"That's enough for me."

Gault closed his fist around the cigarette stubs. At the moment they were more important to him than all the gold in the world. "Before we do anything, we'll have to go back and see about Torgason."

"Not me," Wompler said firmly. "I can smell that gold; I'm not goin' to let it get away from me now."

CHAPTER TEN

Torgason lay exactly as he had the last time Gault had seen him. "No sign of the rifleman," Gault told him. "There's some tracks down by the cottonwood—three horses, maybe a mule. And these." He dug the cigarette stubs out of his pocket and showed them to Torgason.

The stock detective studied them with a weak grin. "I know what you're thinkin', but it's loco. Wolf Garnett's back at the New Boston graveyard."

"Somebody's back there. Identified as Wolf Garnett by Wolf's sister and two old pals. But I'd still like to see the man who smoked these cigarettes and bunked on Esther Garnett's sleepin' porch." He hesitated a moment, then asked, "Can you help me, Torgason?"

Torgason laughed silently. "I didn't think you came back all this way just to help a busted-up range detective. You and Wompler have got a sickness, Gault. But I'll make a bargain with you. Fix up my leg best you can, leave me a full canteen and promise to send me some help first chance you get—and I'll tell you what I know. It ain't much."

Gault nodded. "It's a bargain. Is the body in New Boston Wolf Garnett?"

"Far as I know. But I can't prove it." He closed his eyes

and let his thoughts move through curtains of pain. ". . . Still, there's somethin' queer goin' on. It ain't like Esther Garnett to just pick up and quit that farm. She'd have to have good reason to do a thing like that."

"The gold?"

Torgason bared his teeth in what might have been a grim smile. "The longer I lay here, the less I think there's any gold. It was a fever in our brains—mine and Wompler's anyhow." He sighed to himself and tried to move his shattered leg.

Gault showed his disappointment. "Is that all you've got to tell me?"

"One more thing. When that farm wagon went into the river and Shorty Pike got his head busted, it was no accident. Oh, Shorty was pitched off the wagon seat, all right, and was throwed into the water. But he never hit no rock. That wasn't what caved in his head."

Gault squinted. "What did?"

"A piece of one of the bows that was holdin' up the wagon sheet. I found it wedged under the wagon box when I found the body. One end of the bow was bloody and it just fit the dent in Shorty's head."

"In the fall he could have been thrown against the bow; it could still have been an accident."

Torgason was shaking his head. "That broken piece of bow had been pulled out of the bracket, held by the busted end and swung with considerable strength."

Gault quietly considered the story and, for the moment, accepted it. "Why didn't you mention this at the time?"

"I work for the Association, and anything I find out is Association business. Anyhow, at the time I was still thinkin' about the gold. I figgered Esther Garnett seen her chance to get a bigger part for herself, so she yanked out that oak bow and smashed Shorty's head while he was in the water. It looked like she was doin' all of us a favor by gettin' Shorty out of the way. . . . But since that time I've been layin' here thinkin'."

"Thinkin' what?"

"I've decided she didn't do it."

Gault stared at him.

"That *she* didn't do it," Torgason repeated. "The sheet was up; we don't know who was in the wagon besides her and Shorty." He watched the look of understanding come over Gault's face. "You've got me doin' it now," the detective said dryly. "Everywhere I look I'm beginnin' to see Wolf Garnett. Of course," he added quickly, "that's not the only way it could of happened."

Woodenfaced, Gault waited.

"It might just be that Wompler's suspicions about the sheriff are right. He could have caught up with the wagon as it went into the river and finished Shorty off hisself."

"Why would Olsen kill his posseman?"

"Maybe he was makin' it one less way to divide up the gold. You'd have to ask the sheriff about that."

✦

It was late that afternoon when Gault overtook Wompler on the upper reaches of Cashe Creek. The former deputy's eyes were glittering with excitement, "I picked up their tracks almost an hour ago. They're up there somewheres . . ." He pointed toward the heavy timber that bordered the creek. "I've been figgerin' it out while you was away. The place where the gold escort was robbed ain't more than half a day from here. They must of hid the gold here along the creek somewheres, figgerin' to come back for it when some of the excitement wore off. That's what they're doin' now—goin' after that gold!"

Never a question about Torgason. Wompler's one thought was of the gold.

They were dismounted, leading their horses through the

heavy underbrush, when the attack came. It hit with a fury that for a moment left them stunned. Within the close confines of the creekbottom the roaring of rifles was almost deafening. Bullets ripped through the weeds and brush like a slashing rain. One lead slug snatched the hat from Wompler's head and hurled it over the bank into the water. Another bullet nicked Gault's buckskin; the animal reared in panic, jerked its rein free and disappeared into the brush. But not before Gault had hauled his Winchester out of the saddle boot.

Wompler was shouting something, but the sense of what he was saying did not penetrate Gault's consciousness. He threw himself to the ground, scrambled to a thicket of sumac and fired at puffs of gunsmoke on the upper bank. He ducked again into the thicket and crawled upstream on his hands and knees. There was no sign of Wompler, but he saw the black gelding racing ahead of them and disappearing in the timber.

Then, as suddenly as it had begun, the firing stopped. Gault lay in what he hoped was a covered position, listening to the almost silent rustle of new leaves and, from some unseen place nearby, the furious cursing of Harry Wompler.

After a moment Gault called quietly, "Wompler, are you all right?"

"Fine and dandy," Wompler said in a cold rage. "There's a bullet hole in my leg, I lost my hat, and my horse ran off with my rifle."

"How bad are you hurt?"

"I'm still alive, but maybe not for long." Then, grudgingly, "Not bad, I guess."

It was hard to believe that either of them was still alive. Apparently, the rifleman on the upper bank had decided that they were dead, or at least out of action. From beyond a gaudy thicket of redbud, Gault heard someone say, "They're done for. Nobody could of lived through a crossfire like that."

Gault recognized the voice immediately; it belonged to young Deputy Finley. Then, from some unseen position to the right of the redbud, Sheriff Grady Olsen said flatly, "The horses lived through it." After a meaningful pause, he added, "We'll work our way down toward the water. Shoot anything that moves."

The sheriff of Standard County had declared himself. He was a murderer. He had sent an ambush, the single aim being to kill Wompler and Gault. It was not easy for Gault to believe—but it was a fact, harsh and ugly, and it was not likely to go away.

Slowly, like a bull buffalo rising up in a mud wallow, Grady Olsen rose up in a stand of pale green weeds. His rifle was to his shoulder, the muzzle moving snakelike, back and forth, searching the creekbottom for the enemy. Until now Gault had not thought of himself as the sheriff's enemy. Antagonist, perhaps. Or opponent, in this dangerous game that they were playing. But it was no game now.

Not any more. Gault, gazing fixedly up through a curtain of underbrush, could see that rifle muzzle, like one-eyed Death, searching the creekbottom for *him.*

Moving with great care, Gault began actuating the lever of the Winchester and then realized that the hammer was already cocked and a cartridge in the barrel. Cautiously, planning the move inch by inch in advance, he brought the weapon to his shoulder.

From his hiding place, Wompler spoke anxiously, "Do you see him, Gault?"

"Yes." Not much more than a whisper.

"He's out of short-gun range. Have you got your rifle?"

"Yes. Be quiet now."

Apparently Olsen had not seen Gault's gunsmoke. Or, if he had seen it, he didn't know whether it was Gault or Wompler. For that matter, there was no reason for the sheriff to know that Torgason was out of action, unless he had been watching their backtrail. A dead horse didn't necessarily mean a dead rider.

"Gault." It was Wompler again.

"Be quiet."

"Over to the right of the redbud. I think it's Finley."

Gault turned his gaze to the right of the redbud but could see no sign of the deputy. There were a few moments of silence. Olsen was still scanning the creekbottom.

Then Wompler exploded again with suppressed anger. "What're you waitin' on? Kill him! With Olsen out of the way, Finley'll lose interest in the sport soon enough!"

"Shut up!" Gault said through clinched teeth.

Olsen's head came up, his eyes slitted. He made a slight movement with his right hand and then, completely unexpectedly, he ducked into the brush again and disappeared. Gault could hear Wompler cursing disgustedly, and this time he couldn't blame him. He had had Olsen dead in his sights. A slight pressure on the trigger would have removed the threat. And killed a man.

That was the trouble, Gault thought grimly. He was a cowman, not a killer.

Wompler was hissing again between his teeth. "Gault! Do you see him?"

Gault was instantly alert. He scanned the area on both sides of the redbud and saw the movement—a very slight one—where Wompler had seen the deputy. "Yes," he said. "All right. Just see if you can be quiet a while."

He could feel himself sweating. The ground was damp and cold, the air was fresh with springtime, with still an aftertaste of winter in it—but he was sweating. Olsen and the deputy were moving in closer with their crossfire pattern.

Over on Gault's right a clump of green mullein trembled. Was it a vagrant breeze mysteriously channeled across that particular part of the bottom, or was it a rifleman? Gault pushed his hat back and wiped his forehead on his sleeve.

"Gault," Wompler hissed. "Did you see that?"

"Be quiet."

For a time they lay like logs, and the creekbottom was silent. No breeze stirred the leaves on the trees or the weeds on the ground. It was an electric silence that set Gault's scalp to prickling. Then, in the midst of that silence, there was an eruption of sound. In Gault's startled ears it sounded as if a boulder had suddenly fallen out of the sky and was hurtling through the underbrush.

It had been a pebble, probably no larger than a man's thumb. Olsen, or possibly Finley, had thumped it into the brush to distract them. The ruse was as ancient as history's hunt—and it still worked.

It was Wompler, not Gault, who reacted first to the noise. He lurched up in the underbrush, swinging his .45 in a wild arc, firing shot after shot at the harmless undergrowth.

He died almost immediately. Olsen and his deputy fired at almost the same instant. For just a moment Wompler looked over at Gault, appalled to find himself at the center of that deadly pattern of fire. Then thunder rolled down through the bottom, and the former deputy fell back into a stand of weeds.

And that, Gault thought with an eerie bleakness is the end of Harry Wompler. And his frustrated ambitions. And dreams of riches.

This strange mood of disinterest had taken hold of him when he saw the bullets tearing into Wompler, and he was hardly conscious of firing the Winchester until he felt the stock leaping against his shoulder. As in a vaguely remembered dream, he saw the dead face of Deputy Dub Finley passing in front of his sights. Going down slowly, like a ship sinking. Or a tree falling. And that, Gault thought again— still in the grip of that eerie detachment—is the end of Deputy Finley. Pony hide vest, fancy pistols and all.

The numbness lasted only a moment. Wompler was dead

and Finley was probably dead, but Olsen was still very much alive. Gault dived for the ground, and knives drove into his wounded side. He tried not to think of the pain. He brought up the picture of a stagecoach going off a mountain road—and the pain was tolerable. He could almost welcome it.

Olsen fired two well-spaced, thoughtful shots into the area where Gault had been, but by that time Gault had scrambled a dozen yards away through the undergrowth. There he crumpled to the damp ground, gasping for breath. He heard the bullets ripping through the weeds. One of the lead slugs struck a rock and went screaming off into the blue-gray afternoon.

For the moment he was helpless. The breath had been knocked out of him; he couldn't even raise his rifle to his shoulder. He did have his covering of tender green leaves, and Olsen still could not be sure whether he was alive or dead. After the two shots, Olsen had again ducked back into the lacy greenery out of sight. The echoing thunder of riflefire slowly died in the bottom. Again an expectant silence settled on the shady undergrowth.

Then Olsen spoke. One quiet, reasonable man speaking to another. "Gault, this is a lot of foolishness. And damn dangerous foolishness, at that. We can't do one another any good like this; what say we try to strike a bargain?"

Gault started to speak, then realized that that was just what Olsen wanted. It was no bargain that the sheriff wanted; he was hoping that Gault would give his position away. Gault inched his rifle to his shoulder.

"Gault," Olsen said threateningly, "you ain't got nothin' to gain by gettin' me sore. Just hold your rifle where I'll know you won't try to shoot me, and we can talk this thing out."

Gault smiled bitterly and gazed at the wall of weeds over the Winchester's sights. Where was the sheriff's voice coming from? On the upper bank somewhere, beyond the redbud. It was hard to tell, with both of them wrapped in blankets of greenery.

The long silence stretched into minutes. To Gault they seemed like hours. Then the sheriff spoke with a sigh, and for the last time. "Don't be a fool, Gault. What has happened has happened; there ain't no way you can change a thing."

Gault said nothing. He hardly dared to breathe. Then, after another long silence, he heard a quiet rustling in the weeds. Olsen was backing out of the creekbottom. He still couldn't be sure whether Gault was alive or dead; but he was pulling out just the same.

From somewhere in that pale green jungle there was the nervous stamping of a horse. After a moment the sound of hoofs faded away to the north. Soon there was no sound at all.

For whatever reason, Grady Olsen had broken off the fight. Long after the sound of Olsen's horse had faded away, Gault lay in the tall weeds, painfully aware of his injured side. He knew in his mind that Wompler was dead, but he told himself that he ought to get up and make sure. Still, he lay there. The bandages had slipped and his side was bleeding again; he could feel the blood moving warm and wet over the point of his hip. Still, he couldn't bring himself to move just yet. There was too much mystery attached to the actions of Grady Olsen. Too many questions yet to be answered.

Automatically, his hands began unbuttoning his windbreaker and shirt and readjusting the bandage, but his mind was on the sheriff. Why had Olsen left the safety of Standard County to venture into Indian country and commit murder? Why had he broken off the fight, knowing that he might be leaving a rifle-armed enemy to dog his backtrail?

Wearily, Gault pushed himself to his knees. "Wompler?"

The former deputy lay back in green weeds spattered

with crimson. His eyes were blind, his ears deaf. Gault turned his gaze toward the upper bank and called uselessly, "Finley?"

The deputy lay face-down in a stand of dark mullein. First Colly, and now you, Gault thought bleakly. Two men he had killed in almost as many days. It was not a comfortable knowledge to live with. For several moments he stood there, dumbly wondering if there was anything else he could do. There wasn't.

He finished buttoning up his shirt and windbreaker. Then he picked up his hat and brushed it off and started climbing the steep grade away from the water.

When he reached the upper bank he sat on a rotting log and tried to get his bearings. Fort Sill was about a half a day's ride northwest. To the east was the Chickasaw Nation, where a U.S. deputy marshal was headquartered—but too far away to be of any help to Gault. Far to the north was the Cherokee Outlet where more cattlemen were leasing grass—again, too far away.

Night was coming down on the prairie, and the horses were nowhere to be found. Gault made his way to the outer fringe of timber and stumbled on to the north for as long as there was light to see by.

At last he sank beneath the darkly gleaming spread of a liveoak tree. In exhaustion he sat for a long while, his mind a blank. Get some rest, he advised himself, while you can. Tomorrow will look better.

After a long while sleep overtook him. Immediately, Martha was with him. With terror in her eyes. Silently begging him to save her. As the stagecoach went off the mountain road.

*

Gault awoke, as always, in a bitter sweat. For a moment he was startled to find himself here on the edge of the prairie. The chill of the night was in his bones. Only with great effort did he pull himself to his feet and stamp some feeling into his legs.

From the direction of the creek he heard a stirring and rustling, the tentative gobbling sounds of wild turkeys about to take flight from their roosting places. With a sudden urgency, Gault dried and inspected his Winchester. Then, moving as quietly as possible, he made his way toward the stream.

The first flight of the great birds was already leaving the bottomland with a frantic beating of wings. Gault went down on one knee and took careful aim. The bark of the rifle sounded excessively loud in Gault's ears—but a handsome young gobbler fell like a rock from an oak branch.

Within a matter of minutes he had the bird spitted and cooking over a small fire. By the time the sun appeared over the green crown of timber, Gault was finishing his breakfast. With a full belly, the new day did not look quite so cold and dismal. The dead men that he had left on the creekbank were distant memories. Even the nightmare—that never-ending nightmare—was less vivid. Now, he thought, if I could only find the buckskin . . .

But that was asking too much. He made himself accept the fact that he would never see the animal again.

CHAPTER ELEVEN

Gault had been walking most of the day when he first caught the smell of woodsmoke on the still air. He followed the scent into the heavy undergrowth near the creek. He was within sight of the still blue water, carefully parting a way through a tangle of wild grapevines, when a voice said, "Stand right still, Mr. Gault. Or I'll kill you."

The voice sounded tireder and flatter than he remembered it. Gault took its advice and stood very still, his Winchester held loosely in his right hand.

"Let the rifle go," Esther Garnett said.

With great reluctance, Gault let the rifle fall into a stand of weeds. It was like parting with an old friend—the one friend that could be counted on when friendship was needed. "Is the sheriff with you, Miss Garnett?"

"Don't you mind about the sheriff. Move back a piece from the Winchester." He started to do as he had been ordered, but she spoke again, sharply. "First, drop your pistol belt."

Gault still had not seen her. She had come up behind him in the underbrush, very quietly. He unbuckled the cartridge belt and let drop the pistol that he had taken from Harry Wompler. There was a rustle of brush and

Esther Garnett hurried in behind him and gathered up the weapons.

"Now you can turn around."

Gault turned and looked into the muzzle of her cocked .45. "You're a stubborn man, Gault," she said wearily. "Most likely it will get you killed before long." Her cheeks looked hollow; there were dark half-circles of exhaustion beneath her eyes. Thornbrush had torn her clothing in several places, and she was far from clean. Still, there was something about her. Gault could understand how men might do unwise and even dangerous things at her bidding. "Stubborn," she said again, "but not loco, I hope. I don' want to have to kill you." She motioned with the cocked revolver. "Turn around and start walkin'. I'll tell you when you can stop."

Gault moved slowly toward the bank of the creek. After a few minutes she said, "Here," and handed him a saddle canteen that she picked up along the way. "Take this and fill it."

Gault climbed gingerly down the clay bank and pushed the canteen into the still water. She said, "I don't guess you've got any whiskey with you."

Gault looked up, surprised. "No."

"Or medicine? Any kind of medicine?"

He shook his head.

"Have you got any tobacco?"

Gault capped the canteen and slung it over his shoulder. When he reached the top of the bank he handed her his tobacco and papers. She took them quickly and stepped back, never letting the muzzle of the .45 stray from the center of his chest. "They're plain papers," he said dryly. "Not wheatstraw, like the cigarettes we saw back on your sleepin' porch. But maybe they'll do."

She looked blank for a moment. Then, with a sudden coldness in her voice, "Yes sir, I wouldn't be surprised if that stubbornness don't get you killed."

At Esther Garnett's direction, they made their way upstream for several minutes. Gault did not speak. There were questions in his mind—bitter and burning questions—but he did not voice them.

They passed the Garnett mule and two horses staked in the bottom. The smell of woodsmoke was getting stronger. Suddenly they came upon a clearing where there was a crumbling shack of poles and rawhide. And the ruins of a field that might, at one time, have been planted in squash or corn. The field was now grown up in weeds, and the shack was falling down. The Indian who had started this primitive farm had abandoned it long ago. But the shack was not unoccupied; a faint loop of hardwood smoke rose up from the clay chimney.

"Go on in the shack," Esther Garnett said, "and I'll think on what I ought to do with you."

He ducked through the sagging doorway, blinking in the sudden darkness. The only light came from the small fire in the corner fireplace. There was no furniture in the room, but Gault made out two loglike objects on the floor. At first he thought they were rolled beds, one large and one small. Then the small roll cried.

Esther Garnett snapped angrily, "You be quiet, boy! I don't aim to tell you again!"

Gault stared from Esther to the small roll, and back to Esther again. "Who is that boy?"

"The army doc's kid," she said impatiently. "Grady Olsen fetched him here this mornin'. He said it was the only way to get the doc here." She waved the revolver at Gault. "Move over to the corner—there by the door. Set down and stay put—unless you're uncommonly anxious to get yourself shot."

Reluctantly, Gault did as she ordered. None of what she had told him about the boy made any sense. Gault settled himself in the corner of the shack. Slowly, his eyes became accustomed to the gloom. The young boy—he could be no more than six or seven—stared at him in panic. He lay helpless on the floor, to one side of the fireplace, bound hand and foot.

Esther caught Gault's look of disbelief and snapped, "He tried to run off. I couldn't have that."

"Why did Olsen bring him here in the first place?"

She glared at him but didn't bother to answer. Her mood changed suddenly, from irritation to gentleness, as she knelt beside the larger figure. "You all right, Wolf? I had to go after water, and it took some longer'n I figgered on."

Gault froze.

"You warm enough?" she asked gently. "I can build up the fire, if you ain't."

The man murmured something that Gault didn't catch. In the dancing firelight he could see the gaunt, bone-colored face and hot eyes. Was it the face of Wolf Garnett? It was a wasted face, burning with fever. Had he at last come to the end of his nightmare?

Gault heard himself speaking in a voice he hardly recognized. "Who was it they buried as Wolf Garnett, back in the New Boston graveyard?"

Esther glared at him and again refused to answer. When Gault started to get to his feet, she grabbed up the revolver and hissed, "If you want me to kill you!"

Gault hung for a moment, as if suspended on wires. Then, very slowly, he eased himself back into the corner. "It *is* Wolf, ain't it? It's your brother?"

She ignored him. He—and the young boy, as well—might never have existed, for all they meant to her. Anxiety mingled with tenderness as she spoke quietly to the figure on the floor. "It won't be long now, Wolf. Grady's comin' with the doc. He'll fix you up fine. You wait and see. Look," she exclaimed, "what I brought you! Cigarette makin's. You want me to make one for you now?"

The man with the bone-colored face moved his head and sighed.

With loving care, Esther Garnett shook tobacco into a paper, rolled it awkwardly and licked it into shape. She lit it from an ember in the fireplace, and put it between the man's lips.

"Wolf Garnett?" Gault asked in a constricted voice.

Esther turned on him in a cold fury. "Of course, he's Wolf Garnett! My brother never lived thirty years just to get hisself buried in a New Boston graveyard!"

The man with the feverish face rolled his head and looked disinterestedly at Gault. "He ain't nobody to fret about," Esther assured him. "A cowman, used to be. Name of Gault. You recollect anybody like that?"

Wolf Garnett's feverish gaze passed wearily over Gault's face. ". . . No." It wasn't much more than a whisper.

Gault sat like stone. *This was the man that had killed Martha.* The thought was a live coal in his brain. He had searched for months and traveled hundreds of miles, driven by the thought of this moment. Yet, he did not move.

When the cigarette burned down, Esther took it out of her brother's mouth. "You want another one, Wolf?"

He shook his head and closed his eyes for a moment, as if gathering his strength. Then he looked at Gault. "What's he doin' here?"

Esther frowned, and then said thoughtfully, "I ain't right sure. I think maybe he's loco, kind of. He claims you killed his wife."

Wolf Garnett did not look surprised or even very interested. "When was this?"

"Nearly a year ago, I think. Shorty Pike was tellin' me. You and some of the boys held up a stagecoach she was in—the coach went off a high road and she was killed."

Wolf Garnett closed his eyes again and mentally plodded back through a year of violence. "I recollect," he said wearily. "So he's been huntin' me all this time, has he?" The thin lips twitched in what might have been a smile. "Kill him."

In the sudden quiet of the shack the crackling woodfire sounded like pistol shots in Gault's ears. Esther Garnett said slowly, "I don't hardly think I can do it, Wolf. I mean, as long as he just sets there, not makin' a fuss or anything . . ."

"Kill him now and you won't have to worry about it later," Wolf advised her. Then, in a tone of utter exhaustion, "But don't let it fret you. Just watch him. Olsen will attend to him when he gets back. . . . Lord," he sighed, "I hurt."

"Grady said he'd bring back some whiskey, if he could find some."

Wolf Garnett stared at Gault with hot, impersonal eyes. "Is he by hisself? There wasn't nobody with him?"

"There wasn't nobody with him, Wolf. Try to get some rest. I'll watch after things till Grady gets here with the doc."

Esther watched Gault over the sights of the cocked revolver. From time to time the boy would whimper. Wolf had closed his eyes again and appeared to be sleeping. When Gault was sure that his rage was under control and that he was capable of speaking calmly, he said, "Who was it they buried under your brother's name, back in New Boston?"

She glared at him. "He wasn't nobody, just a drifter."

"Did Olsen find him dead, like he claimed, or did he kill him?"

Her hesitation was all the answer he needed. ". . . What difference does it make now? He's dead and buried."

"Why? What would turn a man like Olsen into a rogue lawman?"

She smiled coldly. "There are some men, Mr. Gault, that claim I ain't too hard to look at. Me and the sheriff are goin' to get married after . . . all this is over." Then her chilly smiled turned icy. "But I don't flatter myself that he's done all he's done just on account of me."

"The gold."

She blinked, faintly surprised. "You know about that?"

"The watch that Colly Fay had on him when he died. Wompler and Torgason recognized it from my description."

She shrugged with one shoulder. "Now you know everything." She mentally signed his death warrant.

Gault sat very still, looking into the muzzle of the .45. "How bad is your brother hurt?"

She glanced affectionately at that hot, dry face. "I don't know for sure. His horse went off a cut bank one night and fell on him. That was almost a month ago. Shorty and Colly brought him to the farm to mend." She shook her head dumbly. "But he wouldn't mend. And there wasn't nothin' I could do for him. Doc Doolie says he's all busted up inside and there wasn't nothin' he could do for him either. But there's a army doc at Fort Sill that Grady says can fix Wolf up fine. That's where he is now, gone after the doc."

Now Gault understood what the young boy was doing there. He was the doctor's son and they were holding him hostage.

Esther saw the look on his face and said defensively, "We never aimed to hurt the boy; we'll let him go as soon as his pa gets Wolf fixed up."

Gault looked deep into the girl's cool eyes. She refused to believe that her brother was dying; her faith in the miraculous power of an unknown army doctor was calm and unshakable. She believed that the boy would go unharmed and that everything would somehow work out fine. Grady Olsen would engineer their escape out of the country, they would take the gold with them and they would live like nabobs somewhere in that huge land below the Bravo.

"You say that Colly and Shorty brought your brother to the farm," Gault said. "And Olsen says they were workin' as honest drovers at the time."

She smiled faintly. "Grady figgered it sounded better that way."

Gault said patiently, "Do you actually believe that Olsen can steal a boy from an army post like Fort Sill, and then steal the post doctor, and get away with it?"

"Grady wants me a whole lot," she said complacently. "And he wants that gold, too. Whatever needs to be done, Grady will do it."

*

The night wore on. The boy slept fitfully, waking from time to time in fits of terror. Esther Garnett coolly ignored him and kept her unblinking gaze on Gault. Once Gault said, "You've told me what Olsen hopes to gain out of this. But what about the others."

"The others?" She looked puzzled. "Shorty and Colly knowed about the gold. That's what they was after. And Deputy Finley . . ." She smiled an icy smile of recollection. "I'm afraid Deputy Finley had the notion I'd put Grady Olsen off, once we was all safe in Mexico, and marry him."

"I thought maybe it was somethin' like that," Gault said with a grim smile of his own.

Wolf Garnett lay like a dead man, and from time to time his sister would bathe his forehead with a damp rag— but in one hand she always kept the revolver, and the muzzle never strayed more than an inch or two from Gault's chest.

At last the iron-hard light of dawn sifted down on the derelict shack. Outside, there was a waking and stirring of small things that lived near the water. A raucous bluejay shattered the stillness with its chattering. Then, in the distance they heard the sound of horses.

Esther touched her brother's shoulder and said excitedly, "It's Grady; he's comin' with the doc!"

Wolf opened his feverish eyes and looked at his sister. "Is there any of that tobacco left?"

Watching Gault, Esther placed the cocked revolver in

her lap and rolled the cigarette. Wolf smoked in silence, and it seemed to Gault that his face looked even drier and deader than it had the night before. To relieve the oppressive silence, Gault said, "I don't understand why you're goin' to all this trouble because of a doctor. There was Doc Doolie in New Boston—he was lookin' after your brother, wasn't he?"

Esther's eyes narrowed angrily. "Doolie ain't fit to doctor a sick mule. He admitted hisself there wasn't nothin' he could do to help Wolf."

"Still, Doolie was a doctor and a respected citizen of the county. Why would he involve himself with an outlaw like Wolf Garnett?"

Esther answered his question with a shrug and a sneer. "The doc does what the sheriff tells him. Like everybody else in Standard County."

The horsebackers were going around to the back of the shack. Gault mopped a fine bead of sweat from his forehead and looked at the man who had killed Martha. "There's one more thing that bothers me."

Wolf Garnett chuckled dryly. "I bet. You got a right curious turn of mind, Mr. Gault."

"I warned him it was apt to get him killed," Esther said, and her brother smiled.

"Shorty Pike bothers me. The way he died," Gault went on stubbornly. "When me and Torgason and Wompler found the wagon, Shorty was wedged under the box with his head stove in. It wasn't no accident. We found the wagon bow that was used to kill him."

Wolf Garnett sighed. "I'm afraid Shorty Pike was cursed with greed, Mr. Gault. He was bound and determined to get his hands on that army gold. And I guess he would of, too, because me and him was the only ones left that knowed where it was." He closed his eyes, listening to the horsebackers behind the shack. "Tell you the truth, I would of killed Shorty myself, if I'd had the strength. Turned out I needn't of worried about it. Grady Olsen found Shorty addled by the wreck and attended to it hisself."

Gault stared at him. "The sheriff murdered his own posseman?"

Wolf grinned wearily. "Happens all the time, Gault. You'll see."

A figure loomed suddenly in the doorway. Gault turned to see a stocky, plumpish young man in a ridiculous Burnside beard, blinking at the gloom inside the shack. "Timmy?" he said anxiously. "Are you all right?"

The young boy began sobbing. The man stumbled into the room and knelt beside his son and took him in his arms.

"I thought I said we'd have no fires," Sheriff Olsen said angrily, standing in the doorway.

"Wolf was cold," Esther told him defiantly. "Anyhow, who's to see the smoke, way out here on the edge of the prairie?"

"I saw it. More'n a mile away. And the Fort Sill stage road ain't more'n five miles to the north of here." He looked at Gault, obviously disappointed to see that he was still alive. "You die hard," he said grimly. "But I'll fix that." He came on into the shack and dropped a pair of saddle-bags on the floor beside Wolf. "How you feelin'?" he asked the injured man.

"All right, I guess." It was barely a whisper. The hot eyes moved about the cabin. "Gettin' a little crowded in here, ain't it?"

"I aim to thin it out before long," Olsen said meaning-fully, with a look at Gault. He nudged the doctor with the toe of his boot. "Don't fret over the boy. You do your job good and he'll be fine."

The doctor looked up at Olsen. "Untie my son and let him go. I'll do what you want."

"You'll do what we want, and then we'll bargain," the sheriff told him bluntly.

The doctor set his jaw and turned back to his son.

"Everything's goin' to be all right, Timmy. Try to rest, and don't be afraid. I'll be here with you." Reluctantly, he left his son and turned to his patient.

"This here's Doc Sumpter," Olsen told the room in general. "He's had plenty practice fixin' up busted troopers. Before you know it he's goin' to have Wolf fixed up ready to travel. Ain't that right, Doc?"

Dr. Sumpter placed the back of his hand to Wolf's forehead, then began opening his saddlebags. The sheriff hunkered down next to the fireplace and looked hungrily at Esther Garnett. "How did he get here?" Nodding in Gault's direction.

Esther told him how they had met. "I didn't know what to do with him. So I just kept him here, waitin' for you to come back."

"I told her to kill him," Wolf said with a tired sigh. "But you know how women are."

"Never mind," the sheriff said coldly. "I'll attend to it."

The doctor had frozen in the act of laying out his instruments. Olsen and Wolf were discussing the subject of murder as coolly and disinterestedly as another person might discuss the vagaries of Southwestern weather. It was coming to Sumpter—slowly at first, and then with a rush—that they had no intention of letting him and his son go after he had attended the patient.

"Get on with it, Doc," Olsen said impatiently. "The sooner you get him on his feet the better it'll be for all of us."

The doctor glanced quickly at his small son. "You'd better get the whiskey," he said to Olsen.

"I almost forgot, Wolf. I brought you some whiskey from the doc's own stock." The sheriff smiled coolly, rose to his feet and went to get the whiskey.

Dr. Sumpter unbuttoned Wolf's shirt. "Tell me if this hurts." He applied pressure with his fingers near the center of Wolf's chest. The outlaw screamed. It was a shrill, piercing whisper of a scream that shredded the air like a flight of arrows.

Esther Garnett lurched to her feet and shoved the muzzle of her .45 in the doctor's face. "You do that again I'll kill you!"

The doctor, showing a courage that Gault had not noticed before, glanced at the revolver and said, "It's the only way I can tell how badly he's hurt."

"There must be some other way."

"Possibly." Sumpter shrugged. "But this is my way."

Sheriff Olsen stepped through the doorway carrying a bottle of whiskey. "He's the best doc in these parts, according to Doolie," he told Esther. "Besides that, he's the only doc around. Why don't you go outdoors a while, and I'll call you when he's got Wolf fixed up." He uncorked the bottle. "Here," he told Wolf, "take some of this."

At one time during this brief scene, when there were no guns pointed toward him, Gault had started to push away from the cabin wall. Olsen had met the move with a flinty smile. "Try it," the look seemed to say. "It will be the last move you'll ever make."

Wolf drank some of the whiskey and lay panting shallowly. Olsen spoke to Esther again, gently, "Go outdoors now. I'll see that everything's all right."

She took a deep breath, handed him the revolver and nodded reluctantly. "Here," the doctor said flatly, when she was gone. And he touched another place. "Let me know if it hurts."

The probing and the muffled cries and the cursing went on for a small eternity. Suddenly Wolf gasped and went limp. His hot, dark eyes rolled up in their sockets, and for one savage moment Gault thought he was dead.

"Fainted," the doctor said, looking at Olsen. "It's just as well. There's nothing I can do for him."

Olsen's face became a mask. "He's goin' to die?"

The doctor nodded. "He's bleeding to death inside. No

one can help him now." He began replacing his instruments. "Do you want me to inform his wife?"

"His sister," Olsen said absently. His mind was on other things. "I'll tell her, when the time comes. How long has he got?"

"Not long. A few hours at the outside. May I untie my son now?"

"Later." The sheriff had a frustrating problem to solve. If Wolf died now, the secret of the army gold would die with him. Olsen would be a rogue sheriff, dishonored and hunted in his own land. "Can you bring him around so I can talk to him?"

"It would be more humane to leave him the way he is."

"He'll be a long time dead; he can rest then. Bring him around."

The doctor uncorked a small bottle of ammonia salts and held it beneath Wolf's nose. "Listen to me, Wolf," Olsen said with ponderous sincerity. "The doc's got you fixed up now. You're goin' to be fine, but it'll be a day or so before you can travel. So why don't you tell me where to find the gold, and I'll get everything ready . . ."

Wolf was smiling a cold, thin knife-edge of a smile. "I ain't goin' to make it. Is that the way it is, Doc?"

The doctor folded his arms and looked at him and said nothing.

"I'm tellin' you, Wolf," Olsen said quickly, "you're goin' to be fine. But the quicker I get that gold ready to travel, the quicker we can bee-line it to Mexico."

"You want that gold pretty bad, don't you, Olsen?"

"It ain't for me, it's for Esther. You got to think about her, Wolf. It would be mighty hard on a woman, throwed out on her own, without family or money."

"Family? I'm family, Sheriff. And you just told me I was goin' to be fine."

The sheriff was sweating. Wolf Garnett was about to die,

and nobody knew it better than Wolf himself. He was toying with Olsen, enjoying watching him squirm.

The doctor said, "There's nothing more I can do. Let me untie my son."

Olsen's temper boiled over. "You fix up your patient, and the boy gets let go. That was the bargain."

"I told you how it is. I can't work miracles."

"Doc," Wolf told him through clinched teeth, "you better learn. The sheriff wants that gold mighty bad, and he knows he won't get it if I die." The effort of speaking left him breathless. He lay back panting, little rivulets of sweat plowing along his bone-colored face.

The doctor sized up the situation. What at first had been incredible was now a brutal matter of fact. Even if he could save the injured outlaw—which he couldn't—Olsen would still kill him and his son. Alive they would be witnesses, and a rogue sheriff couldn't afford to have witnesses haunting his future. Still, Sumpter reasoned, he might postpone the inevitable if he could make Olsen believe that he was accomplishing something. While there was life there was hope, of sorts. "There is something . . . I don't know how much use it will be to you . . ."

Olsen grinned. "I figgered you'd think of somethin'."

The doctor reached into one of his saddlebags and took out a bottle of brownish liquid. "Liquor morphinae citralis. Morphine, citric acid, cochinel, alcohol, and a little distilled water."

Olsen eyed the bottle dubiously. "What does it do?"

"Relieves pain. It also induces a sense of dreamlike well being. The patient, after taking a few teaspoons of Liquor morphinae citralis often says things that he would not say otherwise."

Olsen digested this slowly. "Why didn't you give him a drink out of that bottle when you seen what kind of shape he was in?"

"I believe your friend has a punctured lung, in which case morphine would only aggravate the condition."

The sheriff thought about it, then nodded. "Give him a drink."

"It could kill him."

"He's goin' to die anyhow. Might as well let him go in peace."

They had been talking back and forth across the body of the injured outlaw, as though he were already dead. Dr. Sumpter stared at the big sheriff and swallowed with difficulty. "Medical ethics would not permit me . . ."

Olsen raised his .45 and aimed it at the doctor's head. "Give him the medicine or I'll kill you."

"Even with the morphine there's no guarantee that he'll tell you what you want to know."

"Give him the medicine, or I'll kill the kid."

The doctor paled. He bent over Wolf and looked into those burning eyes. "You heard?"

"I heard," the outlaw breathed. "It don't make any difference. I don't aim to tell him anything."

"Listen, Wolf," the sheriff said anxiously, "it's on account of Esther, your own sister, that I want that gold."

Wolf grinned faintly. The doctor held the bottle to his lips and he gulped almost half the medicine.

"Give him the rest of it," Olsen said.

"It will kill him."

"Give it to him."

Resignedly, the doctor put the bottle to Wolf's lips again and he gulped until it was empty.

Several minutes passed. The sheriff stirred uneasily. "How long before it takes effect?"

"Not long now."

Wolf's eyes began to glaze. They turned curiously blank, as if an opaque curtain had quietly been drawn over his burning brain. "Wolf," Olsen said impatiently, "can you hear me?"

The outlaw sighed. "I hear."

"You've got to help Esther, Wolf. Think of all your sister's done for you. Tell me where the gold is and I'll see that she never wants for a thing."

"Go to hell, Olsen," the outlaw whispered.

The sheriff flushed. "Don't you care what happens to her?"

Wolf's pale lips twitched in a smile that said plainer than words that his hate for Olsen was stronger than his love for his sister.

"Wolf, listen to me!"

"Goddam you all," the outlaw said faintly but distinctly. It was the last thing he said. He closed his eyes and began gasping for breath. In a fury, Grady Olsen grabbed his shoulders and shook him savagely. But Wolf Garnett was dead.

CHAPTER TWELVE

For Gault, this was the end of the road that he had been traveling for almost a year. Wolf Garnett was dead. There was a taste of gall in his mouth but no satisfaction.

So, at last, Wolf Garnett was dead. He had to believe it now. This was no unknown body in a New Boston graveyard, this was the body of the famous outlaw himself. It took some time to get used to this. For almost a year his single purpose had been to see to the death of Wolf Garnett, and now he found himself without aim or direction. He didn't even care about saving his own life.

At the moment of Olsen's fury he might have jumped the sheriff and, with Sumpter's help, overpowered him. But he had let the chance slip away. Olsen, much quicker to recover, released his angry grip on the dead outlaw and grabbed his .45. "Set easy!" he snarled at Gault. "You too, Doc. Just back off and be quiet a minute. I got to do some thinkin'."

Young Timmy Sumpter began to cry. The sheriff glared at him and the boy fell into a stunned silence. Slowly, Olsen got to his feet and called, "Esther, come here."

Almost immediately Esther Garnett appeared in the doorway of the shack. "Wolf died," the sheriff said with brutal matter of factness, "without sayin' where he hid the gold."

Esther stared at the still form on the floor. She made a small, almost inaudible cry. Then she came rigidly, proudly erect. Esther Garnett was not the kind of woman to grieve in public. "You said the doc was goin' to fix him."

"I'm sorry, miss," the doctor started. But a look from Olsen silenced him instantly.

"He's dead," the sheriff said bluntly. "That's the important thing right now. And we still don't know where to find the gold."

"I don't care about that."

"You will. Later. It would mean a good life for us."

"I don't care."

"Without that gold we're just a pair of outlaws, like your brother was. And most likely we'll end up like him."

She looked at him coldly. "You're scared."

"I ain't in no big hurry to get myself hung, if that's what you mean. Look here . . ." He took a step toward her, and she took a step away from him. "Look here, with that gold in our hands we can be kings of the mountain, in Mexico."

"I don't like Mexico. I never aimed to go there, with you. All I wanted was your help in gettin' Wolf to a proper doctor."

Gault was surprised at the sheriff's bland acceptance of her hatred. "Tell you the truth, I never much figgered you'd go through with it. A pert thing like you, a wore-out old buzzard like me—we'd make a right queer team, to say the best of it." His eyes narrowed and his voice became harsh. "But I do want that gold. And I aim to have it."

"I don't know where it is."

"Much as you and Wolf talked together, all the time he was laid up at the farm, and he never told you?"

"I never asked, and he never said."

Olsen's heavy jaw was set like a steel trap. He looked at Esther for almost a full minute and then said quietly, "You're lyin'. It don't stand to reason that you could go all that time without learnin' somethin' about the gold."

"I don't care about reason. I don't care about you."

"I know." The sheriff nodded ponderously. "You never cared about anybody, except that no-account brother. Wompler and Finley and some of the others never seen that until it was too late. But you never fooled me. You want all that gold for yourself. That's how you are. But you're not goin' to get it."

"How many times," she said with limitless patience, "have I got to tell you that I don't know where it is."

"As many times as suits you, but I won't believe it."

He fell into another brooding silence. Gault had the eerie feeling that they were two actors on a stage, and he was in the audience watching them act out their stilted plot of terror. Although Olsen still had his .45 aimed at Gault, he seemed to have forgotten that Gault was there. Only when Gault tried to move or change his position did the sheriff notice him.

Esther gazed bleakly down at the still form of her brother. There was grief somewhere in the depths of those blue eyes, but it was silent and still, wrapped in many layers of Garnett pride. "I want to bury him myself. Just by myself."

"Maybe later," the sheriff said, his voice taking a cold edge. "After we get it settled about the gold."

"There's nothin' to settle. I keep tellin' you."

Grady Olsen leaned his heavy head on one shoulder and looked at her. Then he swung the .45 in a short arc so that the muzzle was casually aimed at the point of her chin. "Are you thinkin' I won't kill you? Is that what you're thinkin'?" Esther Garnett gazed coolly down the barrel of the revolver and said nothing. The sheriff went on. "I'm finished with lawin', you realize that, don't you? I burned my ships, like they say, and I can't ever go back to Standard County again. All because of you and your brother and that gold that you dangled in my face. Like danglin' a yellow carrot in front of a jackass. But I ain't no jackass, missie. I aim to have my carrot."

"You won't get it from me."

The sheriff sighed. "You got spunk, I'll say that much for you, Esther. You figger that I haven't got it in me to kill a woman—and you're right. It's the way I was raised. So you figger that sooner or later I'll lay my feathers down and run off and stop pesterin' you." He shook his head. "You're wrong."

"Grady," she said stiffly, "Wolf's dead, and he's the only one that knowed about the gold. Go back to Standard County where you belong."

"Too late for that." He gazed angrily at Gault. Then he turned to the doctor. Finally he looked down at the boy. "Tell me where it is," he said to Esther, "and I'll let the boy go. It's too late for Gault and the doc, they know too much. But I'll let the boy go."

"How many times do I have to tell you . . ."

"Tell me, or I kill the boy."

Sumpter stood frozen. Esther Garnett glanced quickly at Timmy; if she had any feeling for the boy, it did not show in her face. "I can't tell you what I don't know."

Gault found himself in a half-crouch, ready to spring. Olsen wheeled on him, snarling, "Set back against the wall, before I kill you here and now!" Then he smiled tightly at Esther and shrugged his big shoulders. "You'd let me kill the whole pack of them, wouldn't you? Even the boy. And you wouldn't say a word." He was getting an idea. Esther could see it forming in that busy brain behind those pale eyes, and she didn't like it. "That brother of yours is the only person you ever care a damn about, and I guess he still is."

". . . Wolf's dead."

"No mistake about that," Olsen agreed, his tone quietly savage. "It don't make any difference what happens to him now—ain't that right? I mean, it don't make any difference how a man's buried, once he's good and dead."

She looked at him with a growing fear. "The dead wants to be buried decent."

Olsen grinned. "What I had in mind was takin' Wolf up the creek a ways and rollin' him into a bed of quicksand that I seen on my way to Fort Sill. No work, no bother for anybody. Everything quick and simple."

Her face went pale. She swayed for a moment, and Gault thought that she would fall. But she pulled herself together, set her jaw and made herself look at the sheriff. "All right," she said in a hoarse whisper. "I'll tell."

"I thought maybe you would," Olsen grinned. This was his moment of victory. He had risked everything—respectability, power, security—because of a woman and a half-dreamed shipment of gold. He had lost the woman; but that didn't matter, because he had never really had her. He had won the gold. That was the important thing now.

"Where is it?"

"Up the creek a ways. I'll have to show you."

"All right." He leveled his revolver at Gault.

Esther Garnett's voice went up in pitch. "What do you think you're doin'?"

"Everybody's got to die, one time or another. Their time is now."

"No." Her chin jutted stubbornly. "Not now. Not here."

Olsen scowled. "I can't leave them alive, with all the things they know."

"Kill them later, somewheres else. I don't want it done here, where Wolf is."

The ways of women, Olsen's look seemed to say, were past all understanding. But with the gold so close at hand he was not inclined to argue. "All right, I'll take them along with us." Now that he thought about it, it was the perfect solution. Three bodies at the bottom of a quicksand bed would be forever lost.

Gault tensed and prepared to shove away from the wall.

Calmly, Olsen pointed his revolver at Timmy Sumpter. "Make a move that I don't like, Gault, and I kill the boy."

Gault looked into Sumpter's frantic eyes and made himself be still. "Now," the sheriff said comfortably, "that's some better. From here on out I'll keep the boy with me. Long as you and the doc behave yourselves the kid stays alive."

*

They made their way upstream on foot, Esther Garnett leading, followed by Gault and Dr. Sumpter. Olsen, with the frightened Timmy Sumpter tucked under one arm like a sack of meal, brought up the rear.

After several minutes Esther stopped and pointed. "There it is."

The procession came to a stumbling halt. Olsen, with Timmy still under his arm, pushed forward impatiently. "Where?"

"There at the overhang." Esther pointed toward a many-layered shelf of slate jutting out from the creekbank. Olsen squinted but could see no sign of the gold. "It's on the underside of the shelf," she told him. "I'll show you."

Gault was beginning to get a strange feeling about this sudden, almost casual surrender of Esther Garnett. He looked at the doctor for verification, but Sumpter only had eyes and thoughts for his helpless son. Impatiently, Olsen motioned them forward. "I don't see anything."

"Wolf hid it under a tarp—most likely it's covered with dirt, after all this time."

The sheriff moved cautiously out on the tiered roof of black slate. Suddenly he dropped Timmy Sumpter and thrust him toward Esther. "You watch the kid, and no monkey business. I'm still the only one here with a gun, in case anybody's forgot."

Esther took the sobbing boy, coolly, with no change of

expression, as she might have accepted a lifeless bundle of rags. Then for just an instant, she looked at Gault. There was a certain glitter in her eyes. Light from the fires of hate that burned inside her, Gault thought. It was a cold, still look that said, *This is your chance Gault. The only one you'll get.*

"I still don't see it," Grady Olsen was saying with the beginning of anger and suspicion. He was bending slightly over the edge of the shelf when Esther Garnett threw herself at him.

Olsen was big and heavy, solid as a stump, and no bit of a woman like Esther Garnett was going to upset him. But it did surprise him. He blinked once, scowling and angry, as he brushed her aside. And then, before he could pull himself erect or fully regain his balance, Gault hit him.

A shower of pain went through Gault's injured side as he drove his shoulder into the small of the sheriff's back. It was like throwing himself at an oak tree. Gault could almost believe that he had taken root to that roof of slate. Nevertheless, in some impossible way, he did move. Gault dropped to his knees, gasping. The sheriff was standing on one foot, clawing the air with his free hand and cursing as he fell backward into the still water.

"Hurry!" Esther Garnett said hoarsely. "Maybe we can get to the horses before he hauls hisself out of the water!"

For a moment Gault looked at the world through the splintered light of pain. Sumpter, blind to everything else, rushed to his son and was holding the boy in his arms, rocking and crooning to him, tears of relief streaming down his dirty cheeks.

Gault pulled himself to his feet and got the doctor and the boy started downstream. "On the other side of the shack, where the horses are!"

But Olsen was faster than any of them would have believed. Somehow he had worked his way to the top of the opposite bank and was cutting off their retreat with riflefire.

Bullets ripped through the green mullein. Esther threw herself to the ground beside a cottonwood log. Gault and the Sumpters dropped a few paces behind. Olsen's voice, wild with rage, came from the other bank. "There ain't no gold under that shelf, missie! There never was! It's a sorry day for the Garnetts that you ever thought to trick me!"

Gault wormed his way through the weeds and lay down beside Esther. "Are all the horses on the other side of the shack?"

She nodded. "We'd stand a chance if we could get to the guns."

Gault searched back in his mind. How far was it to the shack? Four, five hundred yards? It might as well be five hundred miles. Olsen would simply move ahead of them, cross the creek below the shack and wait for them to come into the clearing. Gault inched his way back to the Sumpters and asked, "Is there any chance of help comin' from Fort Sill?"

The doctor, still looking dazed and clinging to his son, shook his head. "I don't think so. Some people saw me leaving with Olsen, but they don't know where we were going."

"No one at the fort knew that your son had been taken?"

Sumpter shook his head. "Timmy had the run of the post; it wasn't unusual for him to wander about the grounds for hours at a time."

"His mother didn't mind?"

"His mother has been dead almost three years."

Gault lay with his face against the cool ground. By this time the doctor and his son would probably be missed; it was even possible that a detail had been sent to look for them. But that wasn't going to be any help. With Olsen and his rifle just on the other side of the creek. "How," he asked, "did Olsen get the boy in the first place?"

Sumpter looked blank. "Olsen just came on the post and

told Timmy that his father wanted to see him. Somebody must have seen them leaving together, but . . ."

"I know." Gault sighed to himself. None of it made any difference now.

On the other side of the creek Olsen was strangely quiet. Was he playing patient sharpshooter, waiting for someone to give his position away? Or had he moved downstream to where the horses were?

Esther Garnett glanced back at him. She was wondering too. Then, cautiously, she began crawling toward the shack. Almost immediately the sheriff opened fire. Esther scrambled to a shallow gully and lay there panting.

"What are we going to do?" the doctor asked worriedly.

Timmy, frightened by the burst of riflefire, began sobbing. "Keep him quiet!" Gault heard himself snarling. Then, in a quieter, gentler tone: "For the sake of all of us, try to keep him quiet." He began inching through the weeds, heading again toward Esther Garnett.

"The sheriff's in love with you," he said, as though he were continuing a conversation that had been going on for some time. "You can still talk to him and get yourself out of this, even if the doc and I can't."

She shot him an icy smile. "The sheriff never was in love with anybody but hisself. He wanted me, maybe, but that ain't the same thing, is it?"

"I guess not. But it's something. It could still save you."

"No." The word had the ring of finality to it.

Gault shrugged. It was her life; if she was bent on throwing it away, he couldn't stop her.

For some time Gault studied the opposite bank of the creek. Like the near side, it was a thicket of budding cottonwoods and weeds. "Is there a place upstream where I could cross over to the other bank?"

She thought for a moment. "There's a rock crossing just above the shelf. Most likely that's how Grady got across after he fell."

"I'm goin' back and see if I can surprise him. Do you think you and the doc can hold the sheriff's interest for a few minutes without gettin' yourselves killed?"

She looked at him levelly. "Grady Olsen ain't an easy man to take by surprise." For a moment she closed her eyes and looked the way she would look in about ten years—slack faced, dull, and in no way desirable. "But if you're bound to try it, I'll do what I can to hold his attention." She lobbed a small pebble into the weeds ahead and instantly a rifle bullet ripped through the spot.

Gault was sweating. It didn't seem possible that he could make it all the way back to the shelf without giving himself away. Esther Garnett was looking at him in a way that gave no indication of what she was thinking. There didn't seem to be anything else to say. Gault nodded and continued his inch by inch journey toward the shelf.

Dr. Sumpter watched him silently. He had the frightened Timmy tucked under one arm, the other hand ready to clap over the boy's mouth if he started to cry.

The way back to that jutting overhang seemed endless. Every weed, every pebble in the path, every dappled bit of shade and dazzling shaft of sunlight had to be considered before every move. Along the way the rifle on the opposite bank fired only once. That might or might not be a good sign. Gault hoped it meant that Olsen was running low on rifle ammunition.

At last he reached the overhang and lay for a moment breathing shallowly. Then he slipped around the slate roof and began easing himself down the clay bank to the water. Progress was much faster now. With a bend in the creek between himself and Olsen, the need for caution was not so great. He slipped into the cold water and found the rock bottom at thigh depth and started toward the far bank.

Intuition must have prompted Esther to cause some minor disturbance up ahead. Olsen's rifle blazed again as

Gault reached midstream. Then, somehow, he was on the bank, caught in a tangle of cedar roots. He parted the roots and made his way to the top of the bank and lay there until he was breathing normally.

The rifle cracked again, sounding muffled and relatively harmless, now that Gault was behind it instead of in front of it. He began moving toward the sound, picking up a stick as he went. It was not much of a weapon—a rotting gnarled end of tree root—but it was better than nothing.

Now he could see the side of the creek that he had just left. The wall of wide, green mullein leaves stood motionless. At least, Gault thought, Sumpter was keeping Timmy quiet. He slanted closer to the water and cautiously parted a tangle of wild grapevines—and it was then that he saw Olsen.

The sheriff was lying on the edge of the bank, patiently watching the other side over the barrel of his rifle. Directly below the sheriff Gault could see the shallow water shimmering like glass over a bed of mud. He eased his way through the maze of vines and lay in the weeds, about twenty yards behind the sheriff.

He lay there for several minutes, wondering how long it would take him to cover that twenty yards, and how much noise he would make doing it. Too long, he decided. And too much noise. The sheriff had only to flip over on his side and redirect the rifle and fire. A younger, quicker man could do it all in one second. It might take Olsen two. It was still too fast.

Gault held his silence and waited for something to happen on the opposite bank. Something that would seize and hold the sheriff's attention for slightly longer than two seconds. The silence became oppressive. Gault became aware of the hissing of his own breathing, and he tried to stop it. Then, quite suddenly, a cluster of mullein on the far bank bent with an unfelt breeze. Or a flipped pebble. Olsen saw it and fired immediately.

Gault was on his feet and running. Grasping his inadequate club, he threw himself the last short distance, just as the sheriff, snarling, was beginning to turn. Gault flailed with the stick. With almost no effort, the sheriff knocked it aside with the stock of his rifle. Gault lunged, driving his shoulder into Olsen's chest as both men grappled for the rifle. Then they were falling.

Slowly at first, in the impossible way of dreams, they went off the edge of the bank, still fighting for the rifle. The Winchester flew off toward the far bank, hung for a moment in the still air, then fell to the water and disappeared. Gault and Olsen, snarling like prairie wolves, splashed onto the shimmering bed of mud.

His face curiously distorted, the sheriff was grabbing for his .45. But Gault lunged at him, and that weapon also flew out of his wet hand and struck the water and disappeared. Both men forgot their hand to hand struggle for the moment and threw themselves at the spreading circles of water where the revolver had disappeared. It was then that they realized that they had not fallen onto an ordinary mudflat—they were already waist-deep in quicksand.

Gault froze. Standing as still as possible, he searched for a root, a vine, anything to hold to until help came from the far bank. There was nothing. The slick water gathered at his hips. He could feel himself going down, inch by inch, and there was nothing he could do to stop it.

Not ten yards away Olsen was thrashing about in a fury. When he stopped at last, panting for breath, he was almost chest-deep in the sucking mud. Esther Garnett appeared on the far bank and looked down at them coldly, unconcernedly. Gault started to speak, but knew instinctively that his voice would be shrill with panic. He made himself pause and take a deep breath, and then he said quietly, "The rock crossing upstream from the shelf is solid. You can cross there with no trouble. When you get on this side, look for a tree with grapevines in it." He pointed. "Over there. It'll take a little time, but we can still get out of here. With the help of those vines."

She looked down at them and didn't move. A chill went up Gault's spine. He made himself stay calm and move as little as possible. "Ma'am," he said hoarsely, "without help we're not goin' to last much longer. What do you want me to do, beg?"

"That wouldn't do no good," Olsen said quietly. "That no-account brother of hers is dead—she don't give a damn about anything now."

She looked at Olsen with an icy smile. "I had it in mind to get Wolf buried just as soon as I could. But I think I'll stay here a while and watch you sink in that mud."

Olsen threw his head back and shouted a word that made her blanch. But she quickly took control of herself. "You said the army doc would fix Wolf up," she accused him. "It was a lie. You just wanted the gold. Well, you won't get the gold now, Grady. Nor the bounty money that you put in for, for killin' that drifter. Go on and sink in the mud; you got it comin' to you!"

Dr. Sumpter appeared beside Esther and stared at them with wide eyes. "What is it?"

"Quicksand," Gault told him quickly. "We're goin' to need your help gettin' out of here."

"What can I do?"

"Take the rock crossing just upstream from the shelf. When you get to this bank, pull down some of those grapevines, just behind us, where we went off the bank."

"What can I do about Timmy?"

Gault felt himself sink another inch. "Bring him with you. The crossin's safe."

"I'll be there as soon as I can."

The doctor disappeared, and Gault turned to the sheriff, sinking a little deeper. "We're done for," Olsen grinned savagely. "Both of us. It'll take that doc till sundown to figger out a way of gettin' them grapevines out of the tree. If he don't turn gutless and decide to forget the whole thing." He looked up at Esther Garnett. The mud was less than three inches from his chin. "It's a shame," he said ruefully, "that things had to work out the way they did."

She looked at him coldly. Suddenly she spat.

The sheriff grinned crookedly, then seemed to lose interest in her. The shallow, slick water was touching his jutting chin. "Don't stir about any more'n you have to," Gault told him. "But keep your hands free. For grabbin' the vine when Sumpter comes."

Olsen turned his head and looked at Gault with a weary grin. "You don't understand me, Gault. I was finished the minute I decided to throw in with the Garnetts. I guess I knowed it at the time . . ." He sank another inch. "But a man gets tired tryin' to live on a sheriff's pay. He wants somethin' better. A pretty woman. And, for once in his life, all the money he can spend." The water had reached his mouth. He tilted his head back to keep from swallowing it. "There was a time when I seen myself as a lucky man. Boss of the county. Lots of folks that looked up to me—or maybe they was just scared of me. I don't know now. But I do know that it was the cowmen—the men with money—that everybody respected. Well, sir . . ." He spat some water out of his mouth. "Well, sir, one day it come over me like a fever. It seemed like I couldn't live another day scrimpin' along on a lawman's pay." He laughed, then ended by coughing on the muddy water. "Anyway," he went on, "you come a long way and waited a long time to find out some things, and it seems like you ought to know. One day Esther came to me with a proposition. I was to get a share of the gold, and her as well, if I'd help her get Wolf to a proper doctor and then out of the country. Funny, ain't it . . . ?"

Several minutes later, when Sumpter appeared on the

bank with a length of tough green grapevine in his hand, Gault's head was the only one in sight.

*

It was two hours later that Gault made himself stop shaking. He scraped off the mud, then rinsed himself off at the rock crossing. He dried himself beside a fire on the creekbank. And finally he was able to think about Olsen without having his insides go cold, and he knew that the worst was over.

The doctor looked at him in a professional way. "You've been through a lot, Mr. Gault. But after a good sleep you'll be a different man."

"I'm a different man already," Gault said to himself, "from the one that landed in New Boston that day not so long ago." He picked up his mud-stained hat and brushed it on his sleeve and put it on his head. "The sleep will have to wait, Doc. I've got another patient for you; stock detective by the name of Torgason. I think maybe he'd appreciate it if we got to him before the sun went down."

Clifton Adams was born in born in Comanche, Oklahoma. He served with distinction in the U.S. Army during the Second World War. After leaving the service, Adams studied creative writing at the University of Oklahoma and began contributing Western fiction to numerous pulp magazines. *The Desperado* (1950) was Adams's first attempt at a Western novel and it turned out to be one of the finest he would ever write. For some years in the pulps Adams had been rehearsing themes from *film noir*, stories in which a malevolent fate often disrupts a person's life and brings a resolution in the most ironical of circumstances. *A Noose for the Desperado* (1951) was a sequel in which Adams pursued this same perspective. These novels and his subsequent work are not populated by heroes and heroines. Some of them do not even have a romance of any kind but, when one does, it is treated convincingly. In many ways Adams's finest achievement remains the group of discreet Western novels he wrote published by Doubleday, beginning with *The Dangerous Days of Kiowa Jones* (1964). This group, right through to the last one, *Hassle and the Medicine Man* (1975), reveals an author of immense sensitivity and intelligence, concerned with the interiors of the souls of his characters. At his best he can generate visceral excitement through the frequent encounters of his characters with the futility of life, the failure of true renewal on the frontier and in its communities, just as he can satisfy the intellectual curiosity of his reader by his assortment of protagonists who find themselves in moral and psychological dilemmas in which they are almost certainly at odds with their instinctual natures and alienated by the crude, violent, often bleak world that encompasses them.